PULP
Literature

Issue No. 18

Spring 2018

PULP LITERATURE PRESS
Issue No. 18, Spring 2018

Pulp Literature Press, Publisher; Jennifer Landels, Managing Editor; Melanie Anastasiou, Acquisitions Editor; Susan Pieters, Story Editor; Jessica Fabrizius, Assistant Editor; Daniel Cowper, Poetry Editor; Amanda Bidnall, Copy Editor; Mary Rykov, Proofreader; Kris Sayer, Graphic Designer; Winston Le, Publicity Intern. For advertising rates direct inquiries to info@pulpliterature.com

Cover painting, *Windseeker*, by Akem. Illustrations for 'Bone Dry' by Ben Baldwin Illustrations for *Allaigna's Song: Aria* by JM Landels. All other illustrations by Mel Anastasiou.

Pulp Literature: ISSN 2292-2164 (Print), ISSN 2292-2172 (Online), Issue No. 18, Spring 2018.

Pulp Literature Press gratefully acknowledges the support of the Canada Council for the Arts.

Canada Council   Conseil des arts
for the Arts   du Canada

Pulp Literature is a proud member of the Magazine Association of BC.

Magazine **BC**
association of

TABLE OF CONTENTS

From the Pulp Lit Pulpit
A Breath of Fresh Fiction   7

Stones
Genni Gunn   9

Feature Interview
Genni Gunn   35

We Come Back Different — Part II
AJ Odasso   39

The Commute
Sophie Panzer   59

Bug in My Ear
Susan Pieters   75

Colour Blind Son
Susan Alexander   79

Stella Ryman and the Mah-Jongg Box
Mel Anastasiou   83

On a Dark Lake's Edge
Angela Rebrec   115

The Brightness of Things
Jessica Barksdale   119

The SiWC Storyteller's Award
Michelle Barker   147

The Raven Short Story Contest
Elaine McDivitt, Kerry Craven   161

Bone Dry
Roy Gray & Ben Baldwin   181

Allaigna's Song: Aria
JM Landels   187

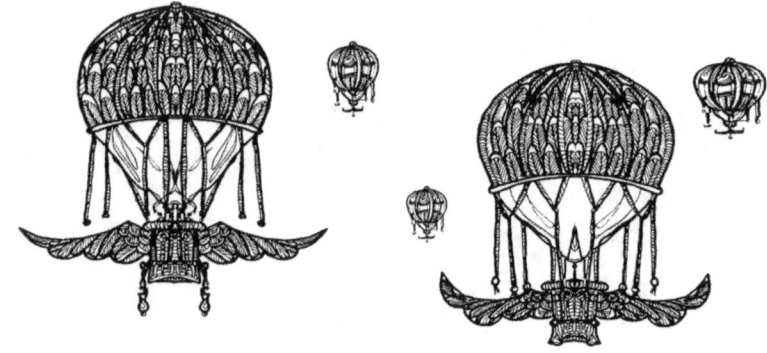

FROM THE PULP LIT PULPIT

A Breath of Fresh Fiction

We at Pulp Literature are always excited to share a new issue of stories with you. When we began the magazine, we decided to publish the stories and poems we would love to read, and we're delighted that you, our valued subscriber, like these gripping tales and intriguing poetry as much as we do.

We struggle to select from the many brilliant manuscripts we receive during each submissions window, to present you with the best in a balance of genre, style, and tone to keep you rapt and reading throughout this springtime, and all year long, in the most beautiful print book and ebook we can devise.

Beneath the beautiful, breezy 'Windseeker' by artist **Akem** we have fresh fiction to begin the new season, starting with 'Stones' by featured author **Genni Gunn**, who makes a tourist confront demons, both personal and cultural, lurking in an ancient Cambodian temple.

What are the chances that out of four million people, Max wins a trip to the moon? But that's only one of a lottery's unexpected outcomes in 'The Brightness of Things' by **Jessica Barksdale**.

With the conclusion of **AJ Odasso**'s 'We Come Back Different', you'll enjoy a page-turning mix of strange science and

mysterious disappearances in an alternate Steampunk past; and poets **Susan Alexander** and **Angela Rebrec** open our eyes to beauty with verse.

Catch up with your favourite heroines as Stella Ryman sleuths out the thief who stole Thelma Hu's fortune in **Mel Anastasiou's** 'Stella Ryman and the Mystery of the Mah Jongg Box'; and in the latest episode of *Allaigna's Song: Aria* by **JM Landels**, our heroine finds herself safely out of the frying pan and well into the fire, with magic her only way to escape.

'Bug in my Ear' by **Susan Pieters** might make you hear something new, and in **Sophie Panzer's** 'The Commute', demons on the Metro mean that being late for work is the least of your problems.

We're not sure whether 'Bone Dry' by **Roy Gray** and **Ben Baldwin** counts as bathroom humour or bathroom horror — either way, this quirky short comic will give you a shiver.

This issue is full of contest winners, with the winner of the Surrey International Writing Contest Storyteller's Award, 'MVP' by **Michelle Barker**, as well as the winner and runner-up of our fourth annual Raven Short Story Contest: 'The Tape' by **Elaine McDivitt**, and 'Meggie' by **Kerry Craven**.

Please enjoy these stories and accept our sincere thanks for subscribing to make this publication possible.

Jen, Mel, & Sue

STONES

Genni Gunn

Genni Gunn's eight books include novels, short fiction, poetry, and memoir. She has also written the libretto for the opera Alternate Visions, produced in Montreal in 2007, and has translated three collections of poetry from Italian. Her novel Tracing Iris was made into a film, and her novel Solitaria was longlisted for the 2011 Giller Prize. She lives in Vancouver and can be found at gennigunn.com.

$\mathcal{S}$TONES

Although a clear and sunny day, no people gathered on the rich green grass, no children's pockets filled with pebbles. No men shifted from foot to foot, no women gossiped. There was no pyramid of stones, no big black box.

The man sat cross-legged on a patch of earth, on the russet bank of what appeared to be a lake but was a moat two hundreds metres wide. He was in his mid-thirties and wore a faded crimson shirt, sleeves rolled up, and blue jeans. His feet were bare. Pond herons wafted in the air in long smooth glides to the surface of still water. Behind the man, a boy splashed waist-deep, collecting pink and purple water lilies. Across the gravel road, an array of vendor stands shimmered in the heat, kaleidoscopic with silk scarves and purses in reds, oranges, and purples, stone amulets to ward off evil, postcards and guide books, and rows and rows of watercolour Brahmas who stared out with stony eyes. The man could have been a tourist, a bas-relief against Angkor Wat's quincunx pediments, which rose into a sunlit sky; a tourist resting, perhaps, in the shade of a banyan tree after a day's trekking through temples, but for the large black plastic bag which lay beside him open and overflowing with empty water bottles.

Sheila saw him first, as she and Vivian rounded a corner, fanning themselves with cultural travel guides, their hair semi-plastered to their heads, their feet sluggish in sports sandals, as they searched for the rental car and driver who had dropped them off at dawn. They were both in their late twenties, child-hood friends who had survived the divides of university and different career paths. Sheila became a junior geologist at a brokerage firm, and Vivian a receptionist for a revolving door of employers. They had been in Cambodia for four days, exploring the recently proclaimed Eighth Wonder of the World, Angkor Wat, the seat of the Khmer Empire when Cambodia was at its height; Angkor Wat, the world's largest religious structure, and the only religious monument to appear on a national flag. Birds circled above them, landed in the banyans and *kapots* whose tubular, aerial roots fell and spread like white hair.

Poised in a wide semicircle around the man were four teen-age boys in jeans and T-shirts. One wore a light windbreaker. They could have been playing a game, so cheerful they were, as each stooped, picked up a stone and hurled it at the man whose arms rose up, whose hands tried to protect his face. The rocks hammered the man's head, his chest, his arms, and legs.

"Stop that!" Sheila said, surging toward them. "What do you think you're doing?"

The boys turned, startled, and seeing her, laughed and continued to pelt the man. She stamped her foot, waved her arms, yelling. One of the boys grew more vicious, adopted a pitcher's wind-up for better, harder aim. The stone cut a welt into the man's forehead. Blood seeped into his eyebrow.

"Come on," Vivian said, tugging at Sheila's elbow. "Let's just go."

Sheila shook her off and gave her a withering look.

Across the street, two shopkeepers emerged from the canopy of their stands. The younger one opened a yellow umbrella against the sun. On seeing the man, they quickly bent to pick up stones. Sheila stood in their path. "Stop! Stop!" she said to the two women. "Are you all crazy?"

The shopkeepers stared at her, frowning. The boys turned to the new scene, stones in hand. One of them said, "*He* crazy," nodding to the man. The boy's black T-shirt read MEGADETH in red letters above a nuclear explosion.

"He's hurt," Sheila said. She walked towards the man and took a tissue from her fanny pack, intending to dab the trickle of blood on his forehead.

The man shrank from her, shaking his head. His arms covered his face. He began to wail. The boys laughed and circled him in a crazy dance. Sheila felt light-headed; she began to hear a soundtrack of parakeets, parrots, cicadas, all chattering, a soundtrack of strident clickings and buzzings. She turned her head, trying to make out the words. Closed her eyes. *The bones cry out ... the flesh calls for blood.*

"What?" Vivian asked.

Sheila opened her eyes. Had she spoken, or had he? "That man ..." she said and bit her lip. "That's what ... he's saying."

Vivian stared at her curiously. "You don't know Cambodian, Sheila. That man is not saying anything. He's crying."

"But I'm sure I heard ..." Sheila looked at the man who was now curved into a ball, his head low on his chest, his arms wildly trying to deflect the stones. Hadn't she?

Her brother's face swam up before her eyes. Brose, disembodied and smiling. I *will not do this*, she said to herself. I *will not*. She took a few deep breaths.

One of the boys mimicked her. "*Bone cry out*," he said, advancing, eyes wide and mocking. "*Flesh call blood.*" He raised his arm and she flinched.

"He possessed," one of the shopkeepers said. "No soul." She picked up another stone and threw it half-heartedly, so that it did not reach the man who moaned and moved his head from side to side, in a wanton rhythm.

"There's something wrong with him," Sheila said. Japanese encephalitis, she thought. All those rice paddies and pigs. Could that have affected his brain? Or war. Or torture. Or family.

The shopkeeper stepped back, as if Sheila had struck her. She shook her head. "He my teacher once," she said. "But now *preay* ... Evil spirit ..." She undid the knot in her rainbow-batik-marbled *sampot*, rearranged and reknotted it around her slim waist. Then, she turned and walked to her stand. The other shopkeeper followed, looking back furtively only once from beneath the yellow umbrella.

"What about karma?" Sheila called after them. "That could be you in a next life."

The shopkeepers continued walking. Sheila turned to the boys.

"This *his* karma," one said. He shrugged and picked up a stone.

Sticks and stones will break my bones ... What of these people, stone-faced, stone-blind, stone-hearted? Were their convictions solid as rocks? Was their stone fear a good neighbour fence or a prison wall? Sheila trekked slowly to the parking lot, trying to understand the incomprehensible, her feet raising red puffs of dust. Vivian trudged beside her, texting the stoning in vivid detail to her girlfriends in Vancouver. Sheila drew out her own cellphone, checked for missed calls or messages, but there were none. Where was Brose? Why hadn't he called? Left long enough, stones age to gems and guard against affection. Held in the hand, a stone is a conscience.

To Sheila's relief, the driver waved to them as they approached. How would they ever have located him among the dozens of taxis and buses and tuk-tuks lined up and waiting for tourists eager for air conditioning and hotel showers? The monument was only accessible on foot, and they were part of a spurt of tourists streaming down the stone causeway a third of a mile long over the moat once filled with crocodiles. They snaked past a row of open restaurants with palm-frond roofs and plastic tables and chairs, dodging restaurant workers' entreaties and vendors trying to sell them the identical guide books they held in their hands. A cow grazed on corn husks at one of the tables, beside a red plastic chair. A humongous blue bus narrowly missed them but left in its wake a wall of coral dust. Two boys cycled past.

"Over here," Mr San called. He held the door open for them. He had been their driver since their arrival, a mid-forties, attractive man with fine bones and a melancholy look in his bleached brown eyes, like a silent film star. Despite the heat, he looked fresh and unruffled in his black trousers and white shirt, sleeves rolled up, unlike how Sheila felt in her white dusty capris and sweaty pink tank top. In the car, she took off her canvas hat and waved it in front of her face. A wisp of straight blonde hair stuck to one corner of her mouth. Mr San handed them each a water bottle and flicked on the air conditioning.

They drove out of the parking complex, past the man who still sat on the ground, a crowd clustered around him. "Why are they doing that?" Sheila said. "That poor man."

Mr San glanced at the scene and shrugged. "Maybe he inherited bad luck. Or maybe," he said, fingering the *lingam* amulet around his throat, "he is possessed by *besach.*"

"What's that?" Sheila asked.

"The spirit of person who have a violent death."

"There must be a lot of those around here," Vivian said.

Sheila looked at him. "You live with this terrible past," she said, "and yet, you stone a man because you think he's crazy?" She shook her head.

"The man is crazy because a demon has taken him. It is too late for him. We must stone the demon before it comes inside us."

Historical, this hunting and stoning of the possessed: easy release for our forbidden thoughts and desires. In the biblical tale, the possessed man had banished himself to a tomb and spent his days crying out and pelting himself with stones so that he was permanently bruised and scarred. The villagers did not dare kill him, convinced the demons inside him were doing the stoning. They chained him repeatedly, put him in ankle irons, but the possessed easily broke out of all. And so all let him roam—they had a scapegoat, and the madman had his life.

In the hotel room, while Vivian showered, Sheila phoned her brother Brose in Toronto but reached a robotically cheerful female greeting. Sheila left one more message, yet another duplicate of countless duplicates she'd left over the past few days, her frequency in direct proportion to her growing anxiety. Her stomach felt queasy, and she reached into her purse for an antacid. Then she lay on her back, fighting the vertigo that threatened to overwhelm her. She had not spoken to Brose since he'd called her three weeks before, his voice slurred and weepy, asking for money. He was thirty-five, her older brother; he was supposed to be the adult she could phone when in need. Instead, she had been sending him cheques for rent, for food, for gas, for whatever this week's excuse was. He was always losing his wallet, or his job, or reality, and she was sick of it. She had told him so the last time he'd called, despite the promise she'd made their mother to look out for him. She'd hung up, fully expecting he'd call her in a couple of days when he was back to normal, although she didn't know what exactly constituted 'normal' for Brose.

She picked up her travel guide and leafed through it. The Khmer Temples rose, glossy in their stone splendour. Demons and deities, defiant, guarded the gates. Three-headed elephants. The turreted faces of Brahmas stared out of their cardinal points, seeing all. Laterite stacked into heads, furrowed and pocked by rain and wind. There was nothing about stoning.

"You've blown the deadbeat off," Vivian said later, when they were walking in the dark up a busy street to find a restaurant. "Be happy about it."

But Sheila did not feel anything close to happiness. She didn't even feel relief that Brose hadn't called and spoiled her holiday. Her brother was a millstone; he was the boulder she was condemned to roll uphill for an eternity. "I hope he's okay," she said. The early evening air hung heavy and humid. Sheila wished she'd worn a dress instead of her jeans. A viscous throng of cars, tuk-tuks and motorbikes clotted the street, their headlights like large fireflies in the dark. Hotel marquees announced *Apsara Dancing* or *Happy Hour*, or *Two for One Dinner Free*, signs glittering in multicoloured fairy lights. A motorbike veered towards them on the shoulder of the road. She and Vivian stood still while it manoeuvred around them. Dust rose into their faces. Sheila was beginning to regret their decision to walk from the hotel. A tuk-tuk would have been much cleaner and safer.

"You did the right thing," Vivian said. She brushed dust off her black dress. Unlike Sheila, she was wearing impossibly high slingback heels that threatened to twist her ankle at every step. "I bet he pulled up his socks and is getting on with it." Motorbikes whizzed past them on the left, on the right, going in every direction.

"Maybe," Sheila said, unconvinced. They stopped at a traffic light and crossed onto a wide paving-stone sidewalk. Up past a dilapidated guest house, a restaurant whose sign boasted *We Do Not Serve Monkey, Snake, Rat, or Dog*, then a right turn onto Sivatha Street, a main artery flanked with restaurants and shops. "He should have called and let me know he's okay," she said.

They passed a vacant building whose front was plastered with ads for designer merchandise — Gucci shoes, Armani suits, Prada purses — all in multiple colours. A few doors down, a tiny internet café squeezed between a bamboo papaya stand and a digital photo shop. A little further on, Vivian stopped in front of a souvenir/naturopathic shop to admire crystals and stones carved into amulets and jewellery. "I love these," she said, pulling Sheila inside. "Let's pop in for a second and have a look."

Sheila smiled and let herself be guided in. Vivian was a good friend; she was trying in her own way to distract Sheila, to keep her from obsessing about her brother, and doing so by appealing to Sheila's penchant for healing stones.

"Just the thing for you," Vivian said, picking up a moonstone beside which was a card outlining its magical properties: *This stone will help psychic power and answer question in a dream.* "You can dream all about Brose tonight." She paid for it and handed it to Sheila, who turned it over and over in her hand, watching blue and rainbow flashes before zipping it into the pocket of her hoodie.

"Too much information," she said. She imagined a dream in which Brose was wandering back alleys, dumpster-diving, doorway-slumbering under windows boarded and graffitied with anti-slogans. Why couldn't he keep a job for more than a month or two? Sure, he was moody, erratic. One day he'd call, excited about a book or a job or a friend, the next he'd be whispering that someone was watching his apartment. She spent countless hours and dollars speaking to him on the phone. She wished her mother were still alive. She'd know what to do. Or maybe she'd simply continue to do what Sheila now felt was a burden. *He needs help*, her mother had said. *Medication, maybe. I don't know. But he's not right.* Sheila refused to consider this as a possibility. They had grown up in the same house, had gone to the same schools, had both grieved the death of their father, and later their mother. Medication is for Americans, she thought. If she could get up at 7:00 am every morning to go to work, so could he.

Later, after dinner at Curry Walla, they wandered to the Temple Club — a double-decker hot spot they'd read about online with an *apsara* floorshow upstairs and cocktails, dancing, and snooker tables downstairs. They, too, were hot and between boyfriends, although while Vivian was careening towards the possibility of romance, Sheila was fleeing from the shackles of her brother.

Downstairs, the club teemed with tourists: young bronzed men in knee-length khaki shorts and baggy T-shirts; young women in jeans or skimpy skirts and halters, their dangly earrings glittering in candlelight. The air a-chatter, polyglot. Sheila and Vivian stood at the bar, rum-and-cokes in hand, dodging arms and legs on the dance floor. Sheila felt warm and slightly buzzing.

Vivian's elbow prodded her side. "Over there," she whispered.

Sheila followed Vivian's nod into the pool room, where two young men hovered, watching others play. They were tanned and blond — probably German or Scandinavian, Sheila thought — with straight white teeth smiling directly at them.

"I'm going to signal them over." Vivian's eyes lowered. "Are you okay with that?"

Sheila shrugged and sipped her drink.

Lukas, Steffen. Tall and lean. Austrian and German. The men stood near them, spieling a quick biography. They'd been here three days. "Canadian," Sheila and Vivian said. "Four days." The sound system obliterated all efforts at talk. Sheila did not mind one bit. She didn't have the energy to ask or answer twenty questions. She didn't really want to know Steffen or Lukas. She only wanted to be alive, here in this place, tonight, without complications. Lukas asked her to dance, and she let him lead her onto the dance floor; immersed herself in the music's seductive rhythms, heartbeats, palpitations. She closed her eyes and conjured notes into the crannies of her brain, a swirling cacophony of overtones to exorcise thoughts. Steffen and Vivian moved to a table, heads close together, speaking into each other's ears. Now and then, they sent rum-and-cokes to the dance floor, which Sheila and Lukas downed, until the bass thrashed a headache into Sheila's brain. She pulled Lukas to one side.

"I need some fresh air," she said, searching in her purse for a Tylenol.

"I'll come too," Lukas said. "Too smoky."

Vivian looked up. "Let's all get out of here," she said, running a hand through her long black hair so that it shimmered and cascaded back down, water over stones. She followed Sheila and Lukas outside. "Let's do something fun."

"Like what?" Steffen asked when they were all standing in the street. He wore new white tennis shoes, their Nike swoosh flashing in the fluorescent streetlights.

A few blocks up, the glow from the night market. A small boy darted across the street from one darkness to another, a baby strapped across his back. Dust rose from a passing taxi.

"I don't know ... Something frightening, something exciting." Vivian was heady, almost jumping out of her Prada peep-toes.

"I've got a headache," Sheila said, but no one paid her any attention.

A near full moon hung in the sky. Up the street, hand-painted signs of bars and restaurants competed for space at the edges of the unpaved road. A tuk-tuk pulled up, and Sheila recognized Mr San straddling his meticulously clean moto, his helmet and black leather jacket incongruent with his fine features and melancholy eyes. Before she knew it, she bowed and pressed her hands together at chest level, as if she were praying. Mr San nodded slightly, but did not return the Cambodian greeting.

"To Angkor Wat!" Lukas commanded, slapping the leather seat, as if it were a horse. Sheila cringed at the tone of his voice.

Mr San removed his helmet and placed it behind him. "It is closed," he said. "I take you tomorrow at dawn."

"We want to go now," Lukas said. "We want to see something scary."

"Wats are sacred," Mr San said. He stared defiantly at Lukas, hands on his knees. Sensitive, Sheila thought, with long fingers. A piano player's hands.

"What about all those demons guarding the gates?" Vivian asked. "They must be guarding against something." She giggled and slipped her arm around Steffen. He grinned down at her, his head like that of a spiky blond porcupine.

Mr San stared at them, unsmiling, inscrutable. In the open V of his shirt, tattooed letters — a *yantra*, Sheila thought, to ward off evil or bullets or grenades. She wondered if he were a soldier or had been in his youth. *The bones cry out* ... Goose bumps raised on her arms. Mr San touched his heart.

"Come on, old man," Lukas said. "We want to see ghosts." He widened his eyes and spread out his arms in mock ghostly gestures.

"All country is filled with ghosts," Mr San said quietly.

"Well, let's go see some, then," Steffen said, helping Vivian into the tuk-tuk, a friendly hand on her ass.

Mr San scowled, and turned away.

"I'm sorry," Sheila said as she climbed up. "We're a little drunk." They were being disrespectful, she thought, in a country where people practised sorcery and witchcraft, where people worshipped and feared a multitude of spirits and ghosts.

Mr San did not respond. He donned his helmet, flicked on the motorbike, and surged down the street.

The two couples sat across from each other: Sheila and Lukas gazed forward, watching the headlight cut a swath through the dark; Vivian and Steffen faced a shifting shadowed past, eyes closed, locked in a kiss.

Sheila could feel Mr San's disapproval and see it in the stony face and large pale eyes staring at her from the rear-view mirror.

"I know a nice dark place," Steffen said. His hand roved up Vivian's skirt.

Sheila sat up straighter and slipped her arms into the sleeves of her hoodie. The stone settled against her stomach. As Mr San picked up speed, a cool wind rose. Lukas slid closer until his thigh was pressed against Sheila's and she had nowhere to go. She shifted her weight to her outside leg, all the while trying not to stare at Vivian and Steffen, who sat across from her, tongues in each other's mouths, hands and fingers exploring each other's bodies.

"Vivian," she said, and her friend opened her eyes.

Sheila tried to motion with her eyebrows, and with her own eyes. They'd only just met these men, for god's sake. She wished she had returned to the hotel.

"Lighten up," Vivian said, winking at her. "You only live once." She closed her eyes and sank back into Steffen.

"Come on," Sheila said. "You're not alone here."

Lukas casually extended his arm along the back of the seat, like a teenager in a movie theatre. Sheila felt his fingers on her shoulder, pulling her closer.

"Let them be," Lukas whispered. "They're having a good time." His breath was hot in her ear. She shivered out of misplaced pleasure, arousal, but also out of discomfort for feeling this. She closed her eyes. Lukas mistook this as an amorous sign and slid his hand around her waist, drawing her tight to him, his lips in her hair.

She made herself remain immobile, unsure what she wanted or felt. How was it that some things were so black and white when she thought about them yet enveloped her in shades of grey when she was inside them? She glanced at Lukas, at his high delicate cheek bones, his blond curls, his green smiling eyes, his lips full and inviting. Then she saw the tuk-tuk driver's eyes in the rear-view mirror.

"Bring on the ghosts!" Lukas shouted into the darkness. Sheila shied from him, turned away, and stared at the black night, at the black jungle hurtling past them. A strange hum circled in her head. She thought she heard wailing, the thud of stones against flesh.

"What's the matter?" Lukas said. "Are you OK?" And she was brought back to herself in the tuk-tuk, with Vivian and two strange men.

"I want to go back to the hotel," she said.

Vivian looked up, as did Steffen, who yelled above the motor, "How much longer?"

Mr San made a forward motion with his arm, to indicate nearby.

"Where are you taking us?" Vivian said, giggling. "Is it scary?"

Mr San's eyes were hard, hollow. Sheila felt them boring through her, judging her. He nodded. She wanted to shake her head, to say ... To say what? That she was better than this? Different? *It's what you do that counts,* she told herself. Brose's words the last time he phoned. Why hadn't he returned her calls? She looked away. Mr San soon turned left onto a less travelled road. The fat moon was high in the sky and shone a wide slash onto palm fronds. The tuk-tuk followed its own beam along the narrow road. They were utterly alone. For a moment, Sheila wondered if the men had conspired with this driver, if she and

Vivian were unsafe. She thought about all the things she'd never do back home. She'd certainly not get into a car with two strangers and head out into the jungle. She turned to look at Lukas, but the darkness was too thick, so she looked up instead at an aggregate of stars, stepping stones across time, across now and tomorrow and yesterday.

The tuk-tuk pulled to the side of the road and stopped abruptly. Mr San turned off the motor, and they were hemmed in darkness. He pointed into what looked like a field, intermittent trees silhouetted in moonlight. To one side, three bamboo huts beside a mountain of trash. "Get out now," he said, his voice tight.

The four of them obeyed, although suddenly they were not laughing.

"What's this?" Lukas said. "Where have you brought us?"

Sheila stared into the field, her eyes growing accustomed to the dark. She could see pebbles, white stones protruding from the soil.

"This really is creepy," Vivian said in a hushed voice. "Let's get out of here."

Mr San stood at the side of the road. "There are your ghosts!" he said. "Go. Now." He pointed once more, his voice charged.

Sheila followed the command of his voice, stepped into the opening between two trees, and stood squinting at the dotted field.

"What kind of joke is this, old man?" Steffen said.

Mr San came around and stood inches from Steffen. "This country," he said, "is graveyard. That field is wet with blood. That earth is full of bones. Go. Go and find your ghosts. They are everywhere." He turned, got on the motorbike, and drove up the road, away from town.

"Great," Lukas said. "Some madman leaves us out in the middle of nowhere." He stamped his foot. "*Scheiße!*"

"Did anyone get his tuk-tuk number? We ought to report him," Steffen said.

"Who does he think he is?" Vivian said.

Up the road, a few feet away, rose a small pagoda with steps leading up its four sides. The three of them walked over and sat on the bottom steps of the side facing the road. "I'm sure he'll be back to get us," Vivian said. "He's probably trying to creep us out. We said we wanted to be scared. Let's sit tight and wait."

Sheila stayed behind, stood perfectly still, listening to the hum and wail inside her head. She could almost make out words. She bent her head toward the sound of ... clicking, crickets ... The din of bells ringing, quarter tones apart, a discordant sound building to unison, like a giant orchestra tuning up. And then a bass drum, beating — or was it her headache pounding — until she thought she heard gunshots, over and over and over. "He's right," she said finally, and they all turned to her. "There are ghosts everywhere. I can hear them."

"Sheila!" Vivian yelled. "Don't *you* start acting crazy like your brother!"

"My brother is not crazy!" she said, thinking *he is*, thinking *there's something wrong with him*, thinking *I should have done something, should have, should have*. Guilt bore a hole in her stomach. She crouched towards Vivian, raised her arms and let out a shriek that sent Vivian, Lukas and Steffen all scurrying up the steps. Then she followed them up slowly, until their backs were up against a plate-glass wall. "There are your ghosts," she said, pointing, and they turned.

Behind the glass, hundreds of skulls stared out of empty eyes.

Vivian screamed, and scrambled down the steps, Steffen and Lukas right behind her. They ran down the road a ways. Sheila watched them, tried to imagine Vivian pelting her with stones, the impossible, only a stairway down.

"You're a freak!" Vivian called out. "This is not funny."

Steffen took a card out of his wallet and opened his cell-phone. "I'll call us another tuk-tuk," he said. "That dude's a maniac." They continued down the road, the sound of their voices growing fainter.

Sheila sat on the top step and stared into the skulls. Of course she knew about Pol Pot, about the killing grounds. Almost two million people starved, tortured, murdered. A few steps away, a stone well contained the ghosts of hundreds of mutilated bodies. It seemed incredible that no one had been charged, that no one would avenge the dead. She lay down on the top step, reached into her pocket, and put the visionary stone in her mouth. It was supposed to give her clarity, to give her, in dreams, the answer to a question. Back home, Sheila's jar of coloured stones guarded against various real or imagined illnesses — smoky quartz for inertia; carnelian for toxicity; tiger eye for indigestion; rhodonite for hypertension; turquoise for sore throat; amethyst for nightmares; lapis for anxiety; pyrite for migraines ... *Where are you, Brose?* She asked, and found herself in the middle of the field, surrounded by vertebrae, sternums, ribs, femurs, tibias, fibulas protruding from the earth — hundreds, thousands of bones, as if they had suddenly rustled to the surface of the field.

A rattling began from the pagoda; the skulls battered the glass, angry ghosts, decapitated, yearning for release. Above the field, the sky was a cumulous of faces, black and white, burning in and out of focus. Men, women, children, with black haunted eyes. They wanted something from her. But what? She pushed them away, but there were more and more and more, until they became a blur of black and white, bones and earth.

"My father is one of those." Mr San's voice rose out of the darkness.

Sheila sat up and looked around her. She was still on the top step, beside the mound of skulls. She could see neither Mr San nor the tuk-tuk. Instead of fear, she felt immensely tired. How could she possibly understand anything, the damage? "I'm sorry," she said, and put her head down on her knees.

"I don't know which one," he said.

"I hear proceedings have started for genocide," she said. "Noun Chea will be on trial. You will have justice, finally."

"Justice?" he asked. "Will they bring back the dead?"

"Maybe they'll ask forgiveness," Sheila said.

"How can they ask forgiveness when they haven't admitted to be wrong?"

"I think my brother is dead," Sheila said. "And it's my fault."

They both sat, silent and still until an owl screeched in a swoop of wings. "They tell us to forget," he said. "But it's like you step in a puddle and get your pants wet. And thirty years later, they have not dried."

The air felt thick and melancholy. "And you?" Sheila said. "How did you escape your father's fate?"

He didn't answer for a while, and Sheila waited, her heart heavy. Presently, he said, "I was afraid to die."

"We are all afraid to die," she said.

He stepped out of the shadows and sat on the bottom step, looking away from her. "If we kill of our own free will," he said, "that's evil. But if we are ordered to …"

"What are you saying?" Sheila said.

"I was afraid," he said.

Late morning, she left Vivian asleep in the hotel, tiptoed out like a regretful lover, holding the door until it clicked shut. She walked to the end of the hall, and the further she was from the door, the quicker and lighter her steps became until she reached the circular staircase, and now she skipped down as though relieved of a great weight. She slipped her hand into her pocket and fingered the smooth face of the moonstone. The previous night swung, turbulent, in her thoughts. She hoped she would not see Lukas or Steffen, or Mr San, whose confession had precipitated this unspooling. How could she be such a terrible judge of character? How could victims and perpetrators live side by side, intrinsically linked, stupefied and cruel? What did she know about this kind of evil? She, who could not help her own brother.

Up the main road, past the manicured gardens of restored colonial hotels, away from the throng of busses and taxis, she drifted until there were no more guest houses, no western restaurants, no bars. Slowly, the paved road disintegrated into a gravel road, and she found herself in the midst of dusty shanty huts with woven walls and open markets whose stands were bloody with the carcasses of animals. Women squatted on the ground shelling nuts, their ragged children scattered around them. The men stared out of haunted eyes—were they all damaged, then? How to escape one's own dark history?

She walked and walked, until in late afternoon, she ducked into an internet café nestled between a palm and an oleander, and emailed Brose. Phoned once again, but this time, got an out-of-service message. She wondered if he kept her phone number folded in his wallet. She googled Toronto hospitals and called each one, asking if her brother had been admitted. An hour later, when she emerged from the internet café, the mentally ill man was sitting by the door, as if he had been expecting her. He wore the same faded crimson shirt and jeans, but from his feet dangled black plastic flip-flops. She wondered suddenly what he might have seen or done as a child. How easy it would be to fall into suspicion, she thought. Neighbours fearing neighbours.

She recoiled from his outstretched hand. "Help," he said.

Did he recognize her? She scrounged in her purse for a wrinkled bill and held it out.

He shook his head, his eyes looking at hers, beyond hers, as if focused on a point inside her.

What did he want? She smiled, but he continued to stare at her, lolling his head from side to side. She walked around him, stepped off the sidewalk, and crossed the street. She needed to clear her head, to make some decision about Brose. She'd fly to Toronto and find him a facility. Or she could bring him back to Vancouver to live with her. Every time she turned, the man was skulking behind her. "Go away," she'd say, motioning him with her hands.

He'd stop.

However, a block up when she turned again, he'd be following. What did he want? She felt her stomach knot.

She hailed a tuk-tuk and felt better as soon as they drove out of the area and back towards the Old Market and restaurants. "Drive around the temples," she said. She wanted to get away from the man, from pressing need. She pulled out her guidebook and flipped through it. Tomorrow, she'd be flying home, and still she had not seen Ta Prohm, the temple that represented how the entire complex of Angkor Wat appeared when the French naturalist Henri Mouhot rediscovered it in 1861 while searching for butterflies and beetles. Whereas the other temples were in the process of, or had been, restored, Ta Prohm, abandoned for three centuries, was reclaimed by the jungle.

They arrived an hour before closing, when most buses were leaving the complex, the air blue with diesel fumes. The driver dropped her off at the west entrance gate. Ahead of her in the distance, the last straggler of a tour group turned a corner, and Sheila found herself alone. Had she seen a black plastic bag in his hand? Above her, four faces carved into a magnificent stone pavilion, their eyes immutable, all-seeing. The King's eyes. What had they witnessed through centuries? If only they could speak.

The sky had begun to cloud, bathing everything in a greyish hue. Sheila took off her hat and used it to dry her forehead. The tour group had evaporated, or maybe it was hovering out of sight behind the rust-coloured rubble that, in the late afternoon light, began to assume sinister shapes. Each massive block had a hole bored into it. A thousand years ago, men had carved those holes, passed rope through them, and then attached the ropes to elephants that dragged the stones from the Kulen hills, forty kilometres to the northeast of Siem Reap, to their present location. She tried to imagine elephants chained, plodding through the hot dusty terrain, through jungle foliage and flooded river beds, their heads bent, their long trunks swirling in the air.

Ducking around the corner to the right, the man—this time she was sure of it—with the black plastic bag in his hand. Her heart fluttered against the cage of her ribs. She looked back at the entrance gate, but it was too far, too deserted, and anyhow, the driver was to pick her up at the east gate. She turned to the left, away from him.

A sound began, like continuous bells chiming, and as she walked, it swelled, until she realized it was cicadas in the enormous banyan tree whose roots clutched a temple wall, separating it from the rest of the structure. As she approached, instead of roots, she saw white fingers elongated to claws, large monsters, parasites, gripping the temple balustrade, like demons come to challenge the faithful, toppling beliefs, toppling God, Buddha, Shiva, in a powerful show of strength.

The man appeared in a doorway in front of her.

Sheila waved him off. She hurried through a portal, teetered over a collapse of blocks, sharp stone edges digging into her sandals. Found herself in a crumbling courtyard, surrounded by the maws of porticoes skewed by the talons of a sacred fig.

The man followed.

Sheila scrambled across and passed through three small temples, delving deeper and deeper into a maze. At every turn, she saw only more rubble, more temples. The man's breath echoed behind her. She stopped and pointed at him sternly. "Go away," she said again. "Go, go."

The man paused: *"Niak teuv naa?"*

She climbed up a wooden stairway to her right and stopped at a terrace. The sun was dropping quickly, eclipsed by thick clouds. All around, sandstone blocks were piled high as if to form an insurmountable impediment, greyish-green with lichen and shadow. She hurried along a cloistered walkway until it ended abruptly in another courtyard, bounded by walls with blind doors and square piers filled with dancing *apsaras*. Her heart was beating hard in her chest. She took deep breaths to calm herself, then began to scramble across the mountain of ruins.

"Why are you running?" Brose said, and she turned, startled.

Her brother stood across from her, leaning against a blind door. He held out his hand. "Why didn't you help me?" he said.

Sheila closed her eyes. "Go away," she said, but her voice lacked conviction. She fingered the stone in her pocket. *Concentrate on something positive*, she told herself, willing a blank screen to the front of her mind. Her apartment back home. But the *besach* pulled at the corners of her screen, skeletal hands ripping, ripping open a basement room, gunshots, a skull falling on the unmade bed. Her heart pounded in her ears. She stifled a call for help, though there was no one. Made herself count slowly to ten. When she opened her eyes, the man stood where Brose had been. But for the black plastic bag, now half-full, she would not have been able to distinguish him from the bilious stones. He advanced toward her, emboldened by their proximity.

"*Please*. I can't give you anything. Go away," Sheila said, louder now, her voice hysterical.

The shadow scurried across a dark row of pillars.

"Go away, I'm warning you," Sheila said, tears springing in her eyes. She leaned down and picked up a stone.

FEATURE INTERVIEW

Genni Gunn

Pulp Literature: *The vividness with which you describe Cambodia renders it almost as much a character as Mr San or Sheila. How did Cambodia become the inspiration for 'Stones'?*

Genni Gunn: The impetus for 'Stones' came during a trip to Cambodia, when I witnessed a mentally ill man being stoned by a group of teenagers, who seemed blissfully unaware of the impact of their actions. Superimposed on the dark dark backdrop of Cambodia's massacres, in a country where even today, victims and perpetrators live side by side suspicious of each other, this incident set me pondering the stupefying idea that everyone, given the right circumstance, is capable of anything. The story is my exploration of one character's descent into darkness and fear in a country that is truly filled with restless ghosts.

PL: *Mental illness features in your story as well, and you show readers an alternative interpretation of this issue through the lens of another culture. Having drawn from both Western and Cambodian views, what were you able to take away?*

GG: While observing this extraordinary event in Cambodia, what struck me is that, while the teenagers were stoning the mentally ill man, nearby shopkeepers hurried out of their shops and also picked up stones, which they threw without hitting the man. In a country that's steeped in superstition and fear, these people were observing the rites — perhaps as a kind of insurance against whatever evil the man represented — but were not invested in harming the man. Fear also permeates our own society when it comes to mental illness. We don't stone people, but we do alienate them in other subtle ways. For instance, not so long ago — up until the 1950s — the mentally ill were often victims of experiments in institutionalized settings.

PL: *Between music, poetry, literary fiction, and translation work, you seem to have a real passion for language in all its forms. Do you consider these separate spheres, or do you find them influencing all of your work?*

GG: Oh they are definitely all intertwined. Translation, for example, connects me to language one word at a time. I spend countless hours inside dictionaries and thesauruses, exploring the literal, cultural, and connotative meanings within each word. Poetry forces me to be disciplined — every word must be exactly the right word; the lines must be compressed and the overall effect luminous. Fiction reminds me that structure is everything: how we tell a story is as important than what we tell.

I write in multi-genres, and I enjoy them all immensely. Some ideas are perfectly rendered as short stories, others expand and become novels; some condense to poems. I work on several projects at once, so I'm never bored or stuck. I write books about things that intrigue me, about questions that I'm trying to answer. I'm interested in human dynamics, relationships, in the function of memory in our lives, and in how we distort memory and recreate ourselves as we age. At their core, I think all my books contain a secret, something to uncover to arrive at a greater truth.

PL: *When you were just starting out with your writing career, how hard was it to break into the publishing world? Comparing that experience to today's publishing landscape, what do you feel has changed?*

GG: When I began to publish, the publishing landscape was extremely different. There was no self-publishing as there is now, and no really large publishing houses. I had a charmed experience with my first two books. I had been working on them simultaneously over a period of about five years, and had been publishing stories and poems in literary magazines. Two different publishers contacted me and asked if I had a full-length work. I happily sent off a novel and a collection of stories and, believe it or not, both were accepted in the same week (although they came out a year apart). Later, I was fortunate enough to secure an agent. The publishing landscape today has changed tremendously. Self-publishing has created an entire new industry—Amazon publishes about 2500 new ebooks a day! Traditional publishers are of two kinds: the big five multinationals, and the smaller Canadian presses. Both are very selective, which means that it is probably more difficult for a first-time author to publish through that route. It's an interesting time, and one that is ever changing.

PL: *You've written in several different genres; what genre (if any) do you feel 'Stones' fits into?*

GG: I think 'Stones' fits into literary gothic perhaps. Or maybe literary travel gothic. I don't tend to try to label my work.

PL: *What are you working on now? Can we anticipate anything new from Genni Gunn in 2018?*

GG: I'm revising a new novel, in the throes of research for another, and am also working on a collection of stories and one of poems. It works for me.

Selected Bibliography

Tracks: Journeys in Time and Place (2015)—Memoir
Text Me (2013)—Poetry translation
Solitaria (2010)—Novel
Faceless (2007)—Poetry
Hungers (2002)—Stories
Tracing Iris (2001)—Novel

WE COME BACK DIFFERENT *Part 2*

AJ Odasso

AJ Odasso *is the author of three award-nominated poetry collections* (Lost Books *and* The Dishonesty of Dreams, *from Flipped-Eye Publishing;* Things Being What They Are, *unpublished and shortlisted for the Sexton Prize) as well as a handful of short stories. She serves as Senior Poetry Editor at* Strange Horizons *magazine. You can find her at twitter.com/ajodasso.*

In part one of 'We Come Back Different' *(*Pulp Literature Issue 17, Winter 2018*), correspondence between two lovers reveals a relationship straining under the miles between Scotland and Bermuda. Tess, gifted with a brilliant mind and lofty scientific ambitions, leaves her ailing father and much younger brother in the care of her lover, Amelia. A poet at heart, Amelia struggles to wait for a woman who spends her time fascinated with reanimating a washed-up corpse. With their relationship cracking under the strain, Tess receives an urgent letter:* "Your father and Trevor are lost at sea. Come home at once."

$\mathcal{W}$E COME BACK DIFFERENT

PART 2

Amelia stood in profile at the window, veiled in a black silk scarf, each sinew in her slender neck precise. Tess closed the front door behind her, refusing to turn from the sight.

Gareth had already made his way around to the back with Tess's trunk and valise so as not to disturb their reunion. Tess exhaled soundlessly and shifted her weight to the opposite foot.

"Thirteen hours," Amelia said. "Thirteen hours and forty-six minutes."

"I'm here now," replied Tess. "I caught the first departure I could."

Amelia came to her arms then, crushing Tess close with a kiss.

"You don't understand," she murmured. "Thought you'd take longer."

Tess's fingers trembled at Amelia's elbows. "What happened?"

"The whale-watch," Amelia said. "Didn't I tell you about it?"

"You did," said Tess, swallowing hard. "Shillingford should've known better."

"The storm was sudden. This early in the season, no one expected —"

"And Shillingford?"

"What of him?"

"Where *is* he? I'll take him to task, don't think I won't!"

"With your father and your brother, Tess! Where else?"

Tess brushed Amelia's scarf back and off her hair. "Have they found ..."

"No," Amelia replied. "No bodies. Not yet."

Tess permitted Amelia to lead her into the kitchen. The staff had gone home hours ago, leaving the battered wooden worktops scrubbed clean of cooking remnants.

Amelia fetched hot water from the hearth, working in silence. Tess accepted the resulting cup of tea but refused to sit down.

"No sign of the vessel, either?" she asked.

Wearily, Amelia shook her head. "None."

"Damn it all." Tess sank into the nearest chair.

"There's no call for foul language," Amelia said, stepping up behind Tess to remove her hat and stroke the shoulder-length spirals of her hair as they tumbled free. "It won't bring them back."

"They're alive," Tess insisted, wiping her nose on her sleeve.

"That's not very likely, my love, and you know it. Please come to bed," Amelia whispered. "I've been so cold without you."

I've been cold for longer than that, thought Tess, nodding into her tea.

They spent two full days in Tess's bedchamber, emerging only to eat and answer the door.

"You *must* have missed me," said Amelia, cradling a ginger and white kitten wrapped in the black scarf to her smooth, bare breasts. There was more mischief in her tone than melancholy.

"Letter writing isn't my strong suit," Tess said, burrowing into the duvet.

"Perhaps I ought to have been sending telegrams all along."

With an inquisitive *mrrrr*, the kitten's warm, slight weight landed on Tess's back.

"One of Artemis's spawn?" Tess grumped, wiggling, attempting to dislodge it.

"No, one of Parvati's," Amelia said, joining the kitten in toying with Tess's hair.

"I ought to spay them," Tess muttered.

Amelia scooped the kitten off Tess's back. "Don't you dare."

Tess sighed and rolled over to face her. "There are too many. We're not a farm."

Amelia's frown deepened, and she let the struggling kitten hop to the floor.

"Your experiment," she began. "Is it —"

"No," Tess said. "Not finished. I must return as soon as I can."

Amelia grabbed a handful of her hair and yanked her up till they were nose to nose. The pain was astonishing, enough to make Tess's eyes water. She grabbed Amelia's wrist.

"Your father and Trevor are missing. You'll do nothing of the sort."

"On the contrary," Tess said. "As soon as they've been found, I shall."

Amelia slumped against the headboard, her arms folded tightly.

"What if they're found dead? What then?"

"Won't happen," said Tess, massaging her aching scalp. "*Can't.*"

"Who's watching your lovely mistress, then? The first-year?"

"Don't be ridiculous. The laboratory's locked, but Lansdowne has a copy of the key. I've asked him to look in now and again, take notes on the progress. It's going well."

"It?" Amelia echoed, her displeasure deepening.

"No longer living," Tess sighed. "As you pointed out."

"So that rubbish about her humanity and giving her a name—"

"Wasn't rubbish!"

"What have you done to her?"

"I've replaced most of her vital organs with fusion-fuelled clockwork. The eardrum repairs and dental work were mostly for show," said Tess. "Like the garnets in her heart."

Amelia blinked down at her, the movement slow and unfocused.

"For show? They'll cut her up all over again to check your work?"

"Only once they've monitored organ function by external means."

Amelia chewed her lip for a few seconds and then slipped out of bed without a word.

"At least I never had to worry about her walking out on me," Tess said to the ceiling.

Tess woke alone to the sound of the doorbell. She couldn't be bothered to don more than a dressing gown, much though it would have horrified both Amelia and her father.

"Ms Barnes, ma'am," said the ginger-haired young officer, handing Tess a folded missive. She shuffled back a few steps, her eyes trained on the scuffed toes of her boots.

Tess scanned the piece of paper and said, "It cannot be them."

The officer cleared her throat. "I fear it appears to be, ma'am."

"What of Shillingford? No sign of him?"

"No. But our searches have been as thorough as we can manage."

"I suppose you'll need me to come with you."

"Yes. And Ms Kingston, if she'll agree to it."

Amelia did, but not without toast and tea.

Tess wondered if they'd both regret eating.

"They're not far," said the same officer forty-five minutes later, meeting them at the perimeter. "We've preserved the scene. You may catch something we've missed."

"Wouldn't count on it," Tess said, cracking a shaky smile. "I'm not usually up at this hour."

"Thank you," said Amelia, taking the officer's hand as she lifted the rope and followed.

"Tide's coming in soon," said the officer, striding ahead of them. "We can't wait much longer. We'll need to take them to the mortuary as soon as we can. Please tell us what you find."

"Damn it all," whispered Tess, stopping in her tracks.

"Ma'am?" asked the officer, still pointing ahead of them.

"Oh, my love," Amelia said, taking hold of Tess's hand.

Her father lay on his back, fine clothing soaked through and his shoes missing, grey eyes staring sightlessly at the sky. Trevor lay curled on his side not a dozen yards off, his eyes closed.

Amelia dropped Tess's hand, finally, and turned her back.

Tess advanced and didn't stop until she'd dropped to her knees beside Trevor. She pulled a pair of gloves from her back trouser pocket, slipping them on with practised ease.

"The calluses on his hands. He's done nothing but play."

"Ma'am?" asked the officer, sounding rather worried.

"His violin," Tess explained. "Never mind."

She examined the arrangement of Trevor's limbs, which was almost too graceful to have been by chance. She tucked a stray curl behind his ear, prodding gently at his neck. The bloating was an uncomfortable sight, but not so far advanced to render her brother unrecognizable.

"Drowned," said Tess, rising, and strode over to her father's corpse.

"Ma'am, there are signs —"

"Wait," Tess said, closing her father's eyes with careful fingertips.

They hadn't washed up in the positions in which they now lay; there *were* signs of interference. Drag marks in the sand. And, next to her father's thigh, one small, shoeless footprint.

Tess marvelled at it, tracing its periphery as if by recollection. She circled both bodies and found more tracks, plus a scattering—the owner had broken into a run—that led up the strand.

"Whoever arranged them eventually veered off into the surf," Tess explained. "Maybe even swam away. I'd be on the lookout for unfamiliar fishing boats if I were you."

"We already have been," said the officer. "Arranged them?"

"It's not murder," Tess said, glancing over her shoulder at Amelia, who hadn't moved. "Someone's shifted them, though, as I believe you've already noticed. Changed their positions."

"There are a lot of early scavengers," said the officer. "They probably moved the bodies to make sure no valuables had got caught underneath. Might've been too scared to report the find."

"How did you learn of them?"

"Beachcomber. Young lady in a cloak and ragged clothes came by the station, said she'd found bodies on the shore. Told us where, but wouldn't lead us."

"Where is she?" Tess asked. "Did you detain her?"

"Gracious, no," said the officer. "She was terrified."

Tess dropped to her knees again next to Trevor, fingering the footprint.

"What did you say she looked like?"

"Slip of a thing. Dark hair back in a knot. Skin as white as mine."

"You didn't recognize her? She's not one of the local fisherwomen?"

"She was so pale," said the officer. "Thin. Looked like she hadn't slept in a week."

"What was she wearing?"

"Cloak. Canvas trousers and linen shirt, stained."

"Footwear?" asked Tess, by now slightly manic.

Amelia was staring, trying to exclude the bodies from her line of sight.

"Barefoot," said the officer. "Beachcomber. What do you expect?"

Tess hardly registered the cup of tea Amelia handed her as she sat brooding.

The police still believed that scavengers had tampered with the bodies.

Let them, Tess thought, startled as some droplets of hot tea hit her thigh.

"You must be careful," Amelia said, pressing a dishtowel to the spots.

"No use," Tess said. "We'll have to invite everyone to the service."

"Not unless your father put that in his will," Amelia pointed out.

"He hasn't," Tess sighed, rubbing her forehead. "But he was well loved."

"By you," Amelia said, kneeling at Tess's feet. "By *us*. It's a family affair."

"For some reason, I'd imagined we'd be on opposite sides of this argument."

"For some reason, you're always underestimating me."

Tess closed her eyes, picturing the footprint. So delicate. *Uncanny.*

"Come back, my love," Amelia said, touching Tess's cheek. "You're distracted."

"The girl who reported them," Tess said. "The police should have detained her."

"Of course they should have," replied Amelia. "Even I know that."

"She might've been the one who moved them."

"Don't judge her too harshly. She was afraid. And very poor."

"Or she knew something," Tess said. "Shillingford might have — "

"Might have what, Tess? Planned it? Plotted to kill your father and your brother in hopes of gaining the family fortune, and confided in some fisherman's daughter while he was at it?"

"She might have been his lover. You know Shillingford."

"Not really," Amelia admitted. "What you're suggesting is mad."

"Maybe," Tess said, snapping her father's ledger shut.

"There," gasped Amelia. "Outside again. The window."

Tess blinked groggily. "What do you mean *again*?"

"I mentioned it yesterday at breakfast. Scratching, creaking. Two nights now."

"Those damned cats," Tess muttered, tugging a pillow over her head.

"The cats don't climb the trellises at night. They're too busy out back."

Tess sighed and tossed the pillow on the floor. "What do you want me to do?"

Before Amelia could respond, a sharp *crack* sounded from beyond the curtains, followed by an eerie, muted shriek. Tess shivered and leapt out of bed, dashing to the window.

Cats didn't make sounds like that. Their vocal chords weren't shaped —

"Sodding *hell*," said Tess, yanking the curtains open just in time to catch the flash of one slim, white arm as whoever had broken the trellis dropped noisily into the shrubs below.

"Tess!" Amelia shouted, getting out of bed. "What are you—"

"Don't follow me," Tess hissed. She fled the room, not even bothering with her boots as she slipped out the front door and raced to stand beneath the bedroom window.

Above her head, the trellis dangled, swaying in the humid darkness.

Out behind the house, several of the cats hissed and screeched.

"Think you're clever," Tess said under her breath, racing onward.

At the garden gate, she found a shovel. She stalked towards the banana grove, wielding it like a spear. Several kittens scattered before her, mewling pitifully.

Beneath the trees, another cat hissed. Not the same as before.

Tess crept beneath the fronds, into thicker darkness. The cat hissed again. Artemis and Demeter crouched at the foot of one of the trees along the high wooden fence, ears twitching. She waved them off with the shovel and squinted upward.

Despite endless leafy obstructions, just enough moonlight filtered through.

It glinted off the intruder's eyes, affording Tess a brief glimpse at her face.

"What kind of foolish *prank*—"

The girl, who looked for all the world like Halcyon, leapt from her perch and cleared the fence with a breathless huff before Tess could even finish making her demand.

By the time Tess managed to hoist herself up to peer over the fence, the intruder was little more than a rustle amidst the grass and menacing wild palms, casting shadows upon shadows.

"**You should** see a doctor," said Amelia, the next morning over breakfast.

"I'm not ill," Tess protested, spreading jam on her toast. "I'm sleep-deprived."

"Then go back to bed and sleep till I wake you tomorrow morning," Amelia said, pouring Tess another cup of tea. "Half the town's going to turn up."

"I thought we had resolved this issue."

"People are clever. Maybe even cleverer than you."

"Fine, then. We'll steal off to Clearwater instead."

"I'd sooner steal off to Admiral's Cave," said Amelia, all sarcasm.

Tess spent her afternoon stitching the two rips that her dressing gown had sustained the night before. She trailed from room to room after Amelia, reluctant to let her lover out of her sight.

Perhaps a swift marriage *was* the best thing. They'd leave Bermuda for good.

"Stop it," Amelia said, looking up from her writing. She was a tableau of perfection seated half-dressed at her desk, black hair piled atop her head. "I can hear you."

"It was your suggestion," Tess said. "I'm merely taking it."

"I'd rather hoped to scare you into responding."

"You no longer wish to marry me, then?"

"That's not it at all. Let's finish grieving."

"Grieving," Tess echoed. "*Are* we?"

"You selfish bitch. Not all of us are blessed with hearts of brass."

"If only," Tess snapped, turning her head to gaze out the window.

They spent the remainder of the day in the same room but did not exchange further words.

At nightfall, Tess crept upstairs and picked clothes for them. Black taffeta for herself, the gown she had worn to her grandmother's burial. She rummaged in Amelia's wardrobe until she found the finely tailored trousers-and-coat set made of heavy brushed silk.

"You'll need a white shirt," Tess said as Amelia came into the room.

"I don't have one," Amelia said stubbornly. "Blue will have to do."

"I can lend you a white one."

"I'll wear my own clothing."

Tess found herself ushered into the corridor, Amelia's door slammed and locked behind her.

Don't follow me, said the note in Amelia's hasty yet elegant hand. The missive had been slipped under Tess's door at some point during the night.

An inspection of Amelia's chamber told Tess that she'd dressed and gone.

The kitchen showed signs of recent use: a loaf of bread half-consumed on the worktop, a pot of butter with a knife stuck in, and a loose-lidded jar of jam. Two teacups sat to one side.

Tess examined the second with a stab of panic. Had Amelia vented to Gareth?

She dressed in a rush, trousers and a button-down shirt, her funeral dress forgotten.

Another frantic search of the house turned up more peculiarities. The urn containing her father's and brother's combined remains was missing, and so was a quarter of Amelia's clothing.

She would have missed the small, muddy footprint in the

front hall if she hadn't taken to pacing. She didn't want to believe her eyes, but, increasingly, it was the only explanation.

What have I done, Tess thought, *that this should even be possible?*

They could be anywhere by now, but, thanks to the missing ashes, Tess had an inkling. And that was only if Amelia had been in control of the situation, only if their unlikely visitor hadn't come armed — heavens, *no*. One did not make tea for an armed intruder, least of all if one were Amelia.

Tess fled the house and didn't look back, hoping the ferry was running behind.

She spent the hour-and-twenty-minute journey from the Cricket Club docks to Grotto Bay battling seasickness made worse by her lurid imagination. Attempting unguided navigation of Admiral's Cave was risky. She buried her face in her arms against the ferry railing.

Please let it be where Halcyon's been hiding.

On her disembarking, the ferryman offered his condolences. On this tiny archipelago, her face was an easy one to recognize. News of the deaths had spread.

The path to the cave had never been signposted, but decades of curious travellers had worn a sandy path into the green under-brush. The foolish went alone at their peril.

She stepped over into the cool darkness, one hand braced on the clammy wall. She stumbled after about six feet on the rough, slimy path, cursing her weak right ankle.

Tess rummaged in her pocket for the torch she'd pinched from an emergency kit on the ferry, discovering that it only had enough fuel for about ten minutes. She made slow progress, stepping around stalagmites, ignoring the fact that the pain in her ankle might indicate serious injury.

Approximately eight minutes later, the torch went out.

Tess dropped it and stumbled again, groping for the slickness of the cave wall. Her ankle throbbed. She smelled salt water not far off, felt the cool stir of air that promised open space.

"There," said Amelia's voice, strained in the darkness. "Told you she'd come."

"Let there be light," said a much lower voice, some stranger's stilted burr.

Halcyon's torch flared to life less than a yard from where Tess knelt.

"She told me you were beautiful," said Halcyon, picking her way soundlessly over the rock formations to crouch beside Tess. "And so you are," she said, framing Tess's face with her free hand, squinting with her lively, *functional* eyes. "Look at you. Perfect."

"My God," said Tess, too numb to move.

Halcyon grinned, and the effect was devastating. Although her pale face was filthy and her dark hair hung ragged, her cheeks had colour. Her skin, once waxen, gleamed with perspiration.

"God had nothing to do with it," Halcyon said, her grin fading quickly. "Tell me, what did you think was going to happen?"

"I wouldn't mind hearing this, either," said Amelia, emerging from where she'd stood hunched behind a large stalactite, her arms folded tightly across her chest.

"The sutures," Tess said, waving one hand at Halcyon's chest. "They haven't ..."

"Burst? No," Halcyon said, grimacing as she rubbed the back of her neck. "I'm healing. You have no idea how badly they itch. Salt water helps a little. Seems I know how to swim."

"Unbelievable," said Tess, breathlessly. "Incredible."

Amelia cleared her throat. "That's not an explanation."

Halcyon narrowed her eyes, inching closer.

Tess flinched. "You were assigned to me," she said. "It was an experiment."

"Do you name all of your experiments?" Halcyon asked.

"How did you know we gave you a name?"

Halcyon removed a grubby, familiar looking notebook from her back pocket.

"Some of the letters got smudged, but here," she said, flipping through with perfectly coordinated fingers. "I'm Alice. At least that's what I've been telling people. I can read, too."

Tess traced the remaining intelligible letters. *A-L-Y* . . .

"Oh," she said. "*Alyce*. But that's not what we named you."

"No?" Halcyon mocked. "Well, I don't care. I like Alyce."

"It suits you," Amelia said to Halcyon, placing a tentative hand on her shoulder.

"She's beautiful, too," said Halcyon—*Alyce*, Tess told herself. "Your Amelia."

"How shall I explain this to Lansdowne?" Tess blurted. "He won't like it."

"Likely he already doesn't," said Alyce. "I terrified your young hanger-on. He was nosing around the laboratory when I woke. The poor boy ran screaming. Meanwhile, I was freezing, disoriented, and in a lot of pain. Where my body remembers a heartbeat, it found burning."

"And you found my notebook," Tess said, letting her head fall back against the cave wall. "You read it. That really ought to have told you everything. What needs explaining?"

"Where I came from," insisted Alyce. "Who I am."

Amelia crouched down beside her. "I tried to explain—"

Alyce threw her off roughly. "Let Tess try, if she can!"

"We didn't know who you were," Tess sighed. "An old man found you on the beach one morning, just like you found my father and my brother. You were dead. Do you understand?"

"Yes," said Alyce, glaring. "So you cut me up, put in some clockwork, and brought me back to life. Is that what you do at your universities?"

Tess gaped at her. "We don't bring people to life. We use bodies for medical research. Organ replacements, tissue regeneration, limb replacements for amputees—"

"Then can you explain this? Explain *me*?"

"You were the only one," said Tess, dazedly.

"I don't think so," Alyce snarled. "I saw a dozen others on my way out."

"No!" Tess pleaded. "You're the only one who ever *woke up.*"

Alyce stared at her, as if she hadn't taken that into consideration.

"You mustn't have read all of my notes," Tess continued, turning pages until she reached the relevant spot. "There are regulations against that sort of thing. We follow a strict code."

Amelia was sitting very still, frowning, her arms braced on her knees.

"Do you mean to tell me—" Alyce ran her fingers across the page, reading, and then turned the page. "This was an accident. All of this. Because you cut into my neck and fixed my teeth and made it so I could hear. And if you hadn't done *that*?"

"You'd be deaf," said Tess, weakly, and Amelia groaned.

"This is why you don't have any friends," she told Tess.

"You don't?" asked Alyce, sounding as bewildered as Tess felt. "Neither do I."

"I told you," Amelia said, reaching for her hand. "You've got me if you like."

"I'm so glad to see that you two have bonded," Tess muttered.

"She's been kind to me," said Alyce, defensively. "Kinder than you."

"Most people are kind," Tess snapped. "What do you want me to do?"

"That's a lie," Alyce said. "No one wants anything to do with me."

The dirt, Tess thought. *The ragged clothes, the mutilation. Of course not.*

"I'm sorry," she said. "I don't know what to do, what do you *want* me to —"

"An apology would be nice," Amelia said, "but that doesn't begin to cover it."

"She's not sorry," said Alyce, dropping the notebook. "Why should she be?"

"Accident or not, the numbskull owes you that much," Amelia insisted.

"Why?" Alyce asked.

Tess couldn't believe it. That Halcyon — *Alyce* — was capable of reason, language, feelings...

"Oh, God, I *am* sorry," she said softly, horrified. "You have no idea."

"I do," Amelia said. "Lansdowne will fail you because your research ran away."

"Not only that, but I'll be put in prison," Tess realized. "I've committed a crime."

Alyce made a frustrated noise and stood up, pacing between Amelia and Tess.

"You didn't defy the law on purpose," she said. "They can't arrest you for that."

"They can try," Tess said. "This has never happened before."

Alyce held the torch up in front of her face, smiling sadly.

"I'm standing here. Even if I'm the first, there may be others."

She's right, Tess thought. *Lansdowne will have a heart attack, assuming he actually believes that boy. But all he knows is that Halcyon is missing, and theft isn't unheard-of.*

"Tess, this is a disaster," Amelia said, rising. "What *are* you going to do?" She wandered back to the stalactite she'd been hiding behind and emerged with a satchel slung over her shoulder.

"Go back, of course," said Tess, wincing as she attempted to put weight on her ankle.

Alyce raced to her side, offering support. She smelled terrible, and there were probably lice in her hair. But *oh, look at her.* She was extraordinary. She was *alive*.

"With her, I suppose," Amelia said, stepping forward to sling Tess's other arm over her shoulders. "You'll have a lot of explaining to do, and I hope you hire a good solicitor."

"No," Tess said as they struggled back into daylight. "With you."

Alyce stole a melancholy glance at each of them, questioning.

"We'll see," said Amelia, her sights set resolutely forward.

*   *   *

2 September 18 —
Flatt's Village

Dear Tess,

I had greatly feared for your safety when I learned that your intentions of returning to Scotland were in earnest. Life for me on these islands has been quiet, but altogether satisfying.

Thanks to your father's generous posthumous assistance, I reside in a modest flat for the time being. I have taken up work at the aquarium, dedicating myself to service of the creatures in their care. I find the concept of captivity cruel, but there is so much knowledge to gain.

I have made enquiries at the university in Hamilton. Once I have gained sufficient experience through my apprenticeship, I should very much like to pursue the marine sciences.

Write to me with stories of your return. Tell me what Lansdowne said when you saw him face to face. Tell me if the undergraduate recovered, or if he still insists he saw what he did see.

Tell me if they indeed believe that Halcyon was stolen. And, most of all, tell me whether or not you will be earning your degree. I will be quite cross if the answer is no.

Tell me other stories, too, if you can bear it—stories of you and your wife.

I do not regret what has happened to us. I might have stayed with you had I come to know you better, had your beloved struck out for other distant shores.

I will carve out a space for myself on this scattered reef. I will explore the caves and greet the parrot fish from behind your old goggles. I will tell Gareth that I met you in Scotland, which is true enough, and I will take kittens and bananas as gifts to his pretty sister.

There are far worse things to have than a clockwork heart.

Yours,
Alyce

THE COMMUTE

Sophie Panzer

Sophie Panzer *studies history at McGill University. Her first chapbook,* Survive July, *is forthcoming from Red Bird Chapbooks. She was a finalist for the 2017 QWF Literary Prize for Young Writers, a 2016 Pushcart Prize nominee, and the winner of a 2015 Scholastic Art and Writing Awards National Silver Medal. Her work has recently appeared in the* Claremont Review, Nasty Wytches, *and* Soliloquies Anthology. *She enjoys musicals and long walks in the woods.*

The Commute

There's a demon in the metro again, which means I'll be late to work for the second time this week.

"This is ridiculous," I hear a woman behind me hiss as a small crowd of harried commuters throngs around the Atwater metro entrance. A sign in French and English reading, "Out of service 6h — 9h due to demonic paranormal activity. We apologize for the inconvenience and thank you for your patience," is affixed to the doors.

"This is the second time this month!" I turn to the source of the voice, a middle-aged woman with a severe haircut and a navy pantsuit. She looks and sounds like my mother, a formidable, wealthy matriarch from Westmount used to getting her own way in her office and on the synagogue board.

"The people who cut funding to the DPAM don't even *live* here," someone else wails. "If they had to deal with this commute, we wouldn't have to deal with this bullshit."

I'm already mentally drafting an apologetic excuse to my boss, Sharon, but I doubt it will do me much good. I'm working as a paralegal in her downtown office because she's an old friend of my mother's. She's not my biggest fan, especially since I turned her son down for prom in grade twelve and called her out for being a tiny bit racist when she said the one black member of our congregation looked like her hair had been attacked by a vacuum cleaner.

I take out my phone and call Katie, the office reception-ist. "Weisenfeld and McCall," she chirps in her annoying WASP-y upspeak.

"Hi, Katie. It's Anya. Could you tell Sharon that I'm going to be a few minutes late?" My voice is hoarse and raspy, betray-ing the fact that I woke up less than twenty minutes ago. "My metro stop is closed for demon extermination."

There's the briefest pause, and her judgement echoes in it. I can almost hear the latent water-cooler gossip: *Did you hear Anya was late again? Sharon's gonna be so pissed. Be nice — I think she just broke up with her boyfriend. Wait, isn't she gay?* "Sure thing," she says amicably. "Good luck."

"Thanks." I hang up my phone and put it back in my pocket. My hand brushes against a crumpled piece of paper. I take it out, thinking it's a bill that I've forgotten about, but I see that it's a receipt from my last dinner out with Chris. I paid, because I felt guilty about what I planned to do during the walk home. I stuff it angrily back in my pocket. I broke down last night and lay awake for hours, sobbing and wondering what the hell I was doing with my life. Hence the late start, hence the wrath of Sharon.

My instinct is to call my older sister, Ariel, and tell her about how comically bad this week is shaping up to be. But it's five in the morning in Seattle, and engineers at Microsoft who actu-ally have their lives together need their sleep. Ari can't function on less than nine hours, while I've always been able to scrape by on six.

I look back at the sign on the door and speculate about what's going on in the station. Is it an infestation like the one they found on the Orange Line last week? Or is it one big monster that requires teams to take down, teams that the under-funded Demonic and Paranormal Activity Maintenance board can't cover?

Demons are an urban problem like bedbugs and roaches. They feed on the emotional refuse of humans — memories and traumas and arguments and dreams — the same way rats feed on garbage. They emit waste and by-products that can cause depression, nightmares, nervous breakdowns, even hallucina-tions. They tend to cluster in places where large concentrations of people have been living for some time. They haunt a lot of old houses — the mansions lining Ave du Pins in the Golden Square Mile are full of them. The smaller ones are harmless enough and fun to torment, like insects.

I've always had a Knack for killing demons. When I'm around one, my fingertips glow ice blue. If I get close enough to one, I can shoot blue-white flames at it until it disintegrates. When I was six, I liked to entertain myself by zapping the small seven-legged creature I found scuttling from corner to corner on my ceiling. It shrieked and spat when the light emanating from my fingertips singed it.

"You should be a demon fighter," Ari said offhandedly one day after I zapped a dark little form flapping around in the corner of her bedroom. I snorted, partly in derision and partly because of the fumes wafting from the polish we were applying to our toenails. In terms of a career choice, demon hunter is a step below police officer and a step above plumber, hovering somewhere around exterminator territory. In Quebec, the industry is heavily dominated by working-class Francophone men.

"What?" she asked. "You're good at it. You've got the Knack and everything. You have no idea what you want to do with your life anyway. Might as well do something you could make good money at."

She was right about that. After a couple of years sitting in political science lectures with pretentious Marxist hipsters who all wanted to become lawyers, I was feeling hesitant about applying to law school.

"You fixed the toilet in our hotel when we got food poisoning in Mexico," I pointed out as I opened a bottle of green polish and began painting my fingernails. "Doesn't mean you're destined to become a plumber."

She laughed and flicked a lock of strawberry blonde hair out of her dark blue eyes. "That was one time! You know it's not the same thing."

I thought of my great-grandparents, who fled pogroms in Russia in the late nineteenth century and came to Canada with little more than the clothes on their backs. My great-grandmother scrubbed floors for a family descended from a wealthy sugar baron. My grandfather peddled rags from a cart at first, saving up to buy his own sewing machine, then his own tailoring shop, then enough to send my grandfather to study medicine. His son, my father, was also a doctor, and my mother was a real estate agent. My distaste for math and affinity for books led them to assume that I was destined to become a lawyer or a professor. I certainly didn't have any better ideas, so I went with it, declaring a political science major that I assumed would result in some kind of legal career.

"What's the point of me being in school for a liberal arts degree if I'm just going to learn a trade?" I asked.

"To expand your mind. And you might use it down the road, who knows?"

I rolled my eyes. "Shut up and pass me the purple."

That was part of our night-and-day shtick—I was crabby, she was upbeat. I was dark, she was light. I was a mess, she had her life more or less together, except when she drank too much and hooked up with women who always told her the following morning that they were actually straight and had just been looking to 'experiment'. When that happened, she locked herself in her room for days and didn't eat unless my mother made her.

Our conversation about me becoming a demon hunter happened a little more than three years ago, before she moved out west. She's always known that she wanted to be an engineer, and I was truly happy for her when she got the job. But the difference in coasts, countries, and time zones makes her feel very far away.

I started dating Chris a few months after she left, during my last year of university. I had never had a serious boyfriend before. He was buoyant and bouncy and carefree, and this infatuated me at first. We ditched classes and club meetings and dinners with our parents to get high and ride the metro to places we had never been before. We had sex in public places, like the woods on the mountain and a Victoria's Secret fitting room. Being around him felt like floating in zero gravity. In his presence, even the most mundane tasks—grocery shopping, doing dishes—dissolved my worries .

It took me a while to realize that he didn't care about anything, that he was completely content with his life in the most irritating way possible. He was smart but not curious, passively absorbing lectures at school and getting A's without trying. He was kind but not passionate, giving money to a homeless person he passed on the street but not joining any cause or group dedicated to fighting poverty. We must have watched hundreds of movies together, and he never cried at any of them. He would fall asleep before the end, his head in my lap, his breath steaming against my thigh in a way that made me feel either utterly at peace or ridiculously horny, depending on my mood.

He assured me that he loved me. At first I believed him, wanting it to be true. But it wasn't long before doubt started gnawing at my stomach as I watched him gazing at his phone at parties, dozing off while I wept during movies like *Still Alice* and *Brokeback Mountain*, staring unmoved at the news while I raged at the interminable stupidity of the world.

"I love you," he said when he saw I was upset, wrapping his arms around me and kissing my neck. Like he believed that was enough to make everything better. I couldn't blame him because that was how it was supposed to work. Love was supposed to make everything okay. There was no way I could tell him that love wasn't enough, that I wanted anger, sadness, some sign that if he were to die tomorrow he would have something to lose.

I called Ari to complain about him sometimes.

"Break up with him," she advised. "He sounds clueless. You deserve someone who shares your values."

"You're right," I said. *Come home,* I wanted to say.

After dinner the other night, I stopped him at the park.

"This is over," I said softly, trying to keep my voice from wavering.

He stood there for a moment, taking it in. Then he nodded. "Okay. I understand. You do what you have to do." We parted ways calmly, solemnly. He even asked if we could still be friends. I felt like screaming, *Fight back, you fucking sheep! Don't let me do this!*

Maybe he cried after. Maybe he punched a wall or broke a window. But I will never know.

The crowd is dispersing, hailing rideshares or taxis or simply running to the next stop. I cringe when I think of the reception that will greet me when I arrive at work, with my eyes swollen and red from crying and my clothes wrinkled because I haven't done laundry this week. I can feel the strap of my messenger bag cutting into my shoulder, weighed down by the four-hundred-page brief I'm supposed to be reviewing. I printed it all out because reading too much on a screen gives me a headache. I have a vision of myself at seventy, walking with a bizarre lopsided hunch from all of the mornings I spent lugging documents in this bag.

A thought flits across my mind. An impulse, an itch. My fingers twitch.

You're good at it. You've got the Knack and everything.

I glance briefly over my shoulder, trying to see if anyone in uniform is poised to stop me from doing what I am about to do. There is no one. I duck under the caution tape and push through the revolving doors into the station.

It is eerily quiet inside. There is no one manning the kiosk, and a dull echo from down the escalator hints at activity on the Honore-Beaugrand platform. I've been on the metro during its latest hours, usually drunk or high, when the stations are practically deserted. It feels utterly surreal, like a dream or the afterlife. I'm thrown off, wondering for the briefest of seconds whether it's Friday night or Wednesday morning.

I smile, thinking of the first time I took the metro without my parents. Ari and I were going to Little Italy just to prove that we could do so without adult supervision. Eight-year-old me was terrified and trying to pretend that I wasn't. Twelve-year-old Ari let me grip her arm tightly as we waited on the platform and pretended not to notice. "Come on." She pulled me forward when the train arrived. "I know exactly where we're going."

I pull out my OPUS card automatically, then think better of it and hop the turnstile, grateful that I've worn leggings and flats instead of the pencil skirt and heels that most of the women in my office wear. Sharon has been subtly urging me to adopt this style since I started back in June. It's October now.

As I descend the stairs I feel that familiar spark in my hands, the pleasant cool tingle lighting up my fingertips from pinkie to thumb. There is definitely something nearby. I wonder whether other people in the area are feeling a headache or a change in mood. Demons don't affect me the way they do other people — it's part of the Knack. Some people have the Knack, little pieces of the supernatural sparking through their veins, and some people don't. My best friend Margo can toast bagels by touching them. Not ordinary sliced bread, just bagels. There was a boy in my fifth-grade class named Phillipe who could knock things over by bellowing, "Down." He had to be in Special Ed because whenever he got angry he trashed the classroom. He didn't reintegrate into normal classes until high school.

This little skill hasn't done much for me except make me the designated demon killer in whatever room I happen to be in. Every friend group or family has a person responsible for killing flies or trapping spiders and taking them outside. My Knack doesn't work on spiders or bees or any creepy-crawly other than demons, and I generally avoid them. My dad is the one who deals with wasps and centipedes. We joke that even after I move out, we'll still call each other with a demon or a bug problem.

It's nice being good at something that doesn't require end-less standardized testing or a certain GPA or sitting in front of a computer for hours every day while my eyeballs slowly fry and my muscles soften to lard. Killing demons is physical and focused in a way that filing papers and editing documents isn't. I wonder if any of my co-workers, when they use a copy machine or open a new package of manila envelopes, get the same kind of thrill I get from perfectly aiming a beam of blue light. Margo is working in an office right now and has told me multiple times that she derives obscene amounts of pleasure from the smells of paper, the feel of new pens, the rainbows of sticky notes.

There is a group of men on the platform wearing hazmat suits and holding stun guns, talking gruffly in French and staring at a dark form hovering over the tracks. One of them catches sight of me and gestures at me to leave. *"Mademoiselle! Vous ne pouvez pas être ici."*

I ignore him and stare at the demon. It's a monster. There's no other word for it. It looks like it's been here for some time, growing fat off the anxieties and griefs and lusts of the tens of thousands of people speeding by in the train cars every day. Its image flickers from globular and slimy to nebulous and vague, from swampy green to oily black. One moment its surface undulates like water, and the next it seems hard and flinty. Only its two red eyes remain constant, glowing dully from its centre.

It's the size of a very large bear or a very small elephant. I have never seen one grow to be this large. I think vaguely of the stories my cousins from New York tried to scare me with back when we were kids, about the monstrous alligators rumoured to live in the sewers of Manhattan, subsisting on sewage and stray cats. This thing would be a match for any alligator. Maybe three.

I don't understand how it stayed hidden for this long. Even in the darkness of the metro tunnels, it seems impossible for something so large and so dangerous to go unnoticed all this time.

Then I see it flash from green to black again, and I wonder if it's a shape-shifter. Those are rare, with the same mythic status as the rats that grew to be the size of cats in the trenches during World War I.

"Miss, you can't be here right now," says the man in the suit, thinking perhaps that I didn't understand his French. "It is very dangerous. Go back upstairs." He glances at my fingers, now glowing bright blue. "Miss?"

In response, I set down my shoulder bag and direct a spurt of flame at the creature.

It sizzles when it collides with its skin, now soft and oily. At first it doesn't scream, or even visibly react. That spooks me. Then it turns slowly and fixes its red eyes on me.

Anya.

I turn, confused, to see who has spoken. Does one of the men on the platform know my name? It isn't a male voice, though. It is high and whispery, like the voice of a child. It takes me a while to understand that it is coming from the demon above the tracks.

No one loves you, Anya.

I have never encountered one that can speak. "Is it in your head too?" I ask the man next to me. He nods grimly.

Your mother and your father are embarrassed by you. They wonder why you haven't moved out, why you're so behind everyone else. So stunted.

"Not true," I say out loud, even though I'm not quite convinced.

Chris was cheating on you. That's why he was always ambivalent.

And suddenly it *is* Chris, his hair and his body and his eyes, and he is hovering above the tracks and holding the hand of a girl with white-blond hair and huge, unearthly blue eyes.

"Shut up!" I raise my arms and send two more streams of flame towards it. Within a split second it looks like a demon again, and its skin goes hard and glossy, deflecting my energy.

I panic — this had never happened before. And how could it know?

Sharon's going to fire you.

How could it possibly know? I can feel the tingling in my hands fading away. I flex my fingers in a gesture I have performed a thousand times, only to find that nothing happens. The men stare at me like I am completely out of my mind.

Then you'll have to get another job in another cube so you can support yourself and take care of your parents when they're old.

The thing floating above the metro tracks has managed to take the one thing I am really good at, the thing I have always been able to rely on, away from me.

You bring your family low.

I pause, stunned.

And you'll die without ever really having cared about anything, without anyone really caring about you.

The demon starts moving towards me, hungrily, like it is anticipating a feast.

Your sister is happy without you.

I can hear shouting around me, a hand gripping my arm.

She doesn't need you.

My vision is going blurry at the edges. I stumble near the edge of the tracks.

She's never coming back.

I feel like I'm about to collapse, but something clicks into place when I hear those words echoing inside my head. The sentiment is too awful, too familiar, to be true.

I blink, and for a moment I can see myself as a scared, sullen child. Ari's fair hair bounces around her face as she gently tugs me forward on the platform.

I shake my head as though I am dislodging water from my ears.

And then I laugh. Long and loud. It has made a mistake. It has articulated my deepest insecurity, my worst fear, and that is when I realize that it is a mirror, not a crystal ball.

The mirage of the two girls standing together on the platform is gone, but feeling is returning to my fingertips. I direct ray after ray of blue towards the creature, refusing to let up. I aim for the same place every time, until cracks begin to appear in its skin. There is something red underneath, dark and hot like magma.

Its voice gets louder and louder in my head, becoming more obvious and desperate, *YOU'RE UGLY YOU'RE FAT YOU'RE GOING TO DIE ALONE YOU STUPID BITCH,* but I ignore it. I have blown its cover. I send volley after volley of blue towards it until its armour finally disintegrates, leaving nothing but a heap of sizzling red mush on the tracks.

A long, high scream pierces the air. It goes on and on and on. I instinctively clamp my hands, still glowing blue, over my ears, even though I know the sound is inside my head.

Then, finally, it stops. All is still.

The men are gaping at me through their masks, uncertain

of what has just occurred. I have no idea what the legality of my actions might be, but I decide I would prefer to leave rather than find out. Before anyone can say anything, I hurry towards the exit and back up the stairs.

I push through the doors and emerge back into the bright October morning. My hands are no longer glowing, but I'm suddenly lightheaded with hunger. Rather than attempt to go to the office, I decide to look for something to eat. The demon was probably right—Sharon is definitely going to fire me. But I don't really care about that anymore.

By the time I realize I have forgotten my bag in the station, I am blocks away. I don't turn back.

BUG IN MY EAR

Susan Pieters

Sue *is a founding editor at Pulp Literature Press and has been known to throw philosophy books across her living room, sometimes ripped in half. For more of her stories, read any issue of* Pulp Literature.

$\mathcal{B}$UG IN MY EAR

He didn't do it on purpose, but then he didn't stop it from happening, either.

I was lying next to him in bed, and the light was on because he was reading a Wittgenstein treatise that should have put him to sleep. But I think that's what drew them. Little creatures, flying to the light. He said, "There's one on your hair." I thought he was going to brush it off. He tried, I guess.

But I heard — no, felt — something drop. Small, like a leaf in a forest. It fell. Knocked off balance. Into my ear.

I sat up. That probably didn't help.

He couldn't see anything. I couldn't feel it anymore. I thought maybe it was gone. I laid back down. He picked up his book.

I heard — no, felt — a movement against my eardrum. The tiniest brush, but I was wobbling underwater against the weight. Like a tickle on the funny bone, my eardrum spasmed.

Was it crawling? Was it a tiny leg? A wing?

Was it trying to get out?

Would it take a bite, dig a hole ...

I went for the cotton swabs.

Would I push it in further?

How much further could it go in?

Were there spaces it could hide?

I swirled the cotton around.

He was there, watching, the whole time. "What does it feel like?" he asked. He tried to take a picture with his camera. He said he couldn't see anything with his naked eye.

"Take me to the doctor," I said.

"Now? Emergency departments don't deal with this sort of thing." He felt my pulse. "Are you sure something's in there?"

The movement had stopped. Maybe it was dead. Maybe it had escaped. Maybe the lights in the bathroom had been bright enough to guide and lure it away.

Or maybe it was wounded, feet mired in earwax, stuck.

We lay back down in bed and he turned out the light. He kissed my cheek, my ear, whispered that he loved me. That he'd never leave me.

Fool that I was, I believed him.

It was years later that the blackened shell fell out on my pillow, hardened like it had been at the bottom of a toaster, shining like it had been through the very flames of hell.

COLOUR-BLIND SON

Susan Alexander

Susan Alexander *is the author of* The Dance Floor Tilts *(Thistledown Press, 2017). Her work has received poetry prizes from the Vancouver Writers Festival (2015),* Grain *magazine (2016), and the township of Whistler (2017). Susan's poems appear or are upcoming in several literary journals and chapbooks across Canada. This poem was shortlisted for the 2017 Magpie Award for Poetry.*

Colour-blind son

Years ago she showed him a copy of Brueghel's
The Blind Leading the Blind and explained
how the artist chose faded pigments
to play up his subject. She insisted
they were almost
seeing the same painting.

Just as she told him that they see
the same world in twilight
and in winter
when the cold hammers down the colour range
to soot and light, to tones of tan and khaki.

It is not important to the young man
that his mother should understand
the palette he inhabits.
He does not tell her
that the riotous hues she sees
are all in her head anyway,
figments of her own particular perception.

Colour-Blind Son

When he brings a girl home for Sunday lunch,
his mother praises
her Titian hair and green eyes, but to him
she is all the soft shading of a wood dove.
She holds a pose and he draws her with charcoal.

Afterwards they walk in November rain
and watch the dark salmon
belly their slow way upstream.
He points out
the texture of river stones, the layers
of fallen leaves and the two deer motionless
who look back at them from the bush.

STELLA RYMAN AND THE MYSTERY OF THE MAH-JONGG BOX

Mel Anastasiou

Mel Anastasiou *writes the Hertfordshire Pub Mysteries, the Fairmount Manor Mysteries, and the Monument Studios Mysteries. As well, she is the author of two illustrated 30-day workbooks on story structure, the steampunk-themed* The Writer's Boon Companion, *and* The Writer's Friend and Confidante. *For news on published and upcoming new works, visit her website, melanastasiou.wordpress.com.*

Octogenarian amateur detective Stella Ryman discovered Thelma Hu's mah-jongg box in Issue 16 of Pulp Literature, *but the fortune inside it was gone. Now Stella's sleuthing talents, nerve, and stamina are challenged when she determines to stop at nothing to get back what is rightfully Thelma's.*

STELLA RYMAN AND THE MYSTERY OF THE MAH-JONGG BOX

CHAPTER ONE

A thought caught Stella Ryman in mid-descent towards her chair under the Corridor Park skylight. It arrived without warning, the way notices used to arrive back in her days as an elementary school librarian. A knock would sound at the door, and a Grade 7 student would present her with a thin sheaf of official papers and the message typed thereupon: "For home distribution: Parents are not permitted to park in spaces reserved for staff members."

The thought was, *If you don't watch out, Stella Ryman, you'll get caught, and last night's adventure might be the last you ever have.*

No more adventures? The words rang in her mind. Resonated. Yet last night's undertaking had gone smoothly, without remark or investigation. The only evidence that anything had changed this morning was tacked up on the cork board that hung on the wall facing her chair and Thelma's.

Stella realized that she had frozen in place above her chair seat, with knees bent as if undecided whether to sit or pray. In this undignified position, she caught the curious gazes of the three members of Fairmount Manor's Greek Chorus, as Stella privately called them.

Iolanthe, Lucille, and Sally the Nodder's eyes flashed behind the glasses they wore for embroidering pictures of edibles onto pillowcases.

Lucille said, "Get a load of our Stella. Will she sit down or stand up? How will she ever choose?"

"I think she must be enjoying her morning dilemma," Iolanthe said. "After all, how many decisions do we make for ourselves in the course of our days?"

"Fewer than cats at a dog party."

"I sometimes ask myself, where would we be without Stella's little problems?"

As kindly as possible, Stella answered, "Bored to death, probably. For one thing, you'd have a lot less fun sewing in Corridor Park if I weren't here to needle."

Stella finished her downward movement to settle into her chair beside Thelma Hu. She crossed her ankles in their stretch socks, as her mother had trained her to sit, to avoid varicose veins. Stella had much to thank Tanis Marie Seton for, including a helpful aversion to self-pity.

At Stella's side, Thelma Hu sat hunched in her chair and chewed silently on the knob at the top of her cane. A single drop of saliva fell like the gentle rain from heaven upon the tile floor between Thelma's red silk slippers. Or was it drool? The skylight overhead had been known to leak, so Stella gave Thelma the benefit of the doubt. She looked up at the crisp new motivational poster that somebody had put up on Corridor Park's wall that very morning to replace the *Hang in There, Baby* cat poster

Stella had removed the night before. She had meant to keep the adventure of the stolen poster to herself, but seeing that drop of saliva on the floor between Thelma's feet cut her heart like cheese. In a voice too soft for the Greek Chorus to overhear, she said, "I went on a midnight raid last night, Thelma."

Thelma said nothing, but she stopped sucking her cane.

Stella added, "But you can't tell anybody."

"Who would I tell?"

There went another pang. For, now that Farley Lamoureux had passed out of Fairmount Manor and the world itself, Thelma did not have a soul she cared to talk to. Stella was all she had left.

Stella said, "I couldn't take that kitty poster one more minute, so I waited until the crack of midnight. I crept out of my room, listening for night-shift footsteps."

"Night shift? Huh. One care worker in crepe soles."

"Exactly. You can hear Selena coming two corridors away. I found my way here, ripped the poster off the wall, and hid it under the table in the art supply room across from the staff room."

Thelma said, "I have two questions."

"Shoot them at me."

"What did you do with the poster's thumbtacks?"

"I broke a nail on the first one. I left the thumbtacks be."

"A mistake. Second question."

"Yes?"

"Did you go alone?"

"Yes."

In the silence that followed, Stella came face to face with her own selfishness. She didn't need Tanis Marie Seton to tell her what she should have done.

"I have a question for you, too, Thelma."

"Humph."

"Don't you hate this poster even more than the cat poster?"

"I can't see it." Thelma sounded almost pleased at Stella's gaffe.

"Sorry. It's so hard to remember that you're blind."

"I'm not blind," Thelma said. "I have macular degeneration. So, what does it say?"

"It says, *There's always a reason to smile.*"

"Burn it to the ground."

Stella stifled a laugh. From her seat a couple of yards away, Iolanthe smiled. "Everything all right with you girls and your little secrets?"

"Just talking about old movies, ladies. *The Great Train Robbery.*" Stella lowered her voice. "Tell you what, Thelma. One night very soon I'll knock on your door, and we'll do a silent midnight attack together." She could imagine the clatter of Thelma's cane as they made their otherwise stealthy raid.

Thelma now and then read Stella's mind. "What if they hear us?"

"That's the beauty of it. No danger, no fun."

Thelma sighed. "Well, what can they do to us, really?'

"I think it's nasty to whisper in company," Lucille snapped.

Stella met Lucille's, Iolanthe's, and Sally the Nodder's sharply inquisitive eyes. All day they needlepointed pillowcases and hungered like deprived ruminants for gossip that was always so thin on the ground. Could she not shed a little mercy here as well?

"Thelma and I are ..."

Thelma nudged her with a skinny sharp elbow. "Shh."

"Don't worry," Stella muttered. She continued aloud to the Greek Chorus. "We were wondering what sort of punishments would mean anything to us, here at Fairmount, if they caught us doing something really bad. They can't fine us, because we don't have any money."

Iolanthe said, "They can't keep us after school, because we never go home."

Lucille said, "They can't send us to bed without supper, because that would be more of a reward."

Iolanthe said, "They can't beat us, because we already ache."

Thelma said, "They can't lock us up, because we're already here."

The repartee was taking a gloomier turn than Stella had planned, and the bit of grey sky trapped in the skylight over her head didn't help.

Iolanthe said, "One thing is certain, if there is any adventure to be found, our Stella will dig it up."

"She's a real Sherlock-ette Holmes." Lucille took a swift orange stitch in her pillowcase. She was embroidering a carrot with a nasty grin on its face. "We all admire the way you found Thelma's *empty* mah-jongg box."

"Lucille, we are not ones to talk." Iolanthe's tone was reproving. "Neither you nor I nor Sally here have ever found an *empty* box. Only Stella."

Sally nodded.

Out of the corner of her eye Stella caught sight of Theo's yellow sweater, and then Theo himself, standing on the far side of Thelma's chair, at the turning that led away from Corridor Park. His calm gaze travelled from face to face. Except not to Stella's. He knew quite well she was still angry with him for not telling her he was married to a much younger woman outside Fairmount.

Theo's presence upset her further, and Stella could think of no satisfactory reply to the Greek Chorus. Anyway, they were quite right. She had failed Thelma in the matter of the mah-jongg box. A treasure box is nothing without the money inside it. She bowed her head.

Thelma stirred at Stella's side. "I asked Stella to find my mah-jongg box that had been missing for ten years. She found it."

Theo nodded. The three members of the Greek Chorus exchanged glances.

When Iolanthe spoke, she sounded almost apologetic. "I didn't realize that Thelma had asked you to find the box. That's rather nice of you, Stella."

"And after ten years." Lucille shook her curly head. "None of us was even here then."

Iolanthe sighed. "I think that we must offer our congratulations to Stella. And an apology. We underrated your find. You are a Sherlock Holmes after all."

"Or Miss Marple," Lucille countered. "I like Miss Marple better. More of a hero, *I* have always thought."

And Sally the Nodder nodded.

Stella had never before witnessed such a turnabout here in Corridor Park. Congratulations from the Greek Chorus. *Admiration* from the Greek Chorus. She ought to feel like a million bucks, but she did not. She felt like a phony. She felt like a fool. She rose to her feet and addressed the Greek Chorus, Theo, and Thelma.

"Thank you, but I don't deserve such praise. I found the box Thelma had her fortune in. But I did not find the fortune. I said I would find it, and I will find it."

Theo looked perplexed. "But all that money? Surely somebody must have ... how can I put this politely?"

"Somebody robbed it," Thelma said.

"If I find out who that person was," Stella said, "then they will have to give it back."

Iolanthe's glasses flashed. "Good on you."

Lucille said, "Too bad this is an old age home. Everybody who was here ten years ago is dead."

"Not everybody," Theo said. "It's not possible."

"Even the care workers and the staff have changed," Thelma said.

"How would you know if you're blind?" Lucille asked.

"I'm not blind," Thelma said. "I have macular degeneration."

"She has ears, doesn't she?" Iolanthe said. "The care workers do talk to her, like they talk to us."

Stella turned back to Thelma. "Isn't there anybody you remember from ten years ago?"

Thelma shrugged.

Stella faced Theo. No matter how awkward things were between them, she would ask her question. "Do *you* know of anybody who's been around that long? Somebody who might remember Thelma's first days at Fairmount? Somebody who might have seen something suspicious?"

Theo nodded. "There's one person I knew of, but I haven't seen her around lately."

"Then she's dead," Lucille said.

"I'm pretty sure I would have heard if she was dead. Maybe she's upstairs in Palliative now. She's a real character. Hard work, but not easy to forget. Always wears purple velour suits."

Stella's breath caught in her throat. "Who do you mean?"

Theo screwed up his features and then appeared to remember. "Her name is Cassie. Cassandra Browning."

CHAPTER TWO

"**I seek her here**, I seek her there. I, Stella Ryman, seek her everywhere," Stella murmured more to the corridor walls than to herself as she walked about Fairmount, while the morning wore on towards noon. "Is she in heaven, is she in hell, that *demmed* elusive Mad Cassandra Browning Pimpernel?"

Stella thought she heard a chuckle, but it was just some architectural interior discomfort from the old building, gurgling out of a dusty ceiling vent. She carried on past the activities hall, giving the door a wide berth. Odysseus himself would have had to tie himself to the mast of his ship to avoid some care worker dragging him inside and making him do Healthy Movement to Pat Boone recordings.

One thing was certain, Cassandra Browning would not be in the activities hall. Cassie was a rebel, like Stella herself. As far as Stella could see, Cassie had rebelled herself right past the portal of death and through the other side. Stella wished she could ask Cassie why she had decided to stick around here. She was intellectually interested to know the answer. More than this, she wanted a heads-up, because what if at her own death she were offered a choice to stay and haunt or move on? What if she answered wrongly and ended up haunting the halls of Fairmount forever? Stella had no wish to make such a mistake, and she put it on her mental list of questions to ask Cassie.

When she found her. If she found her. For it had been weeks since she'd communed with Mad Cassandra, and perhaps the ghost had moved on. It would be just like Cassandra to move on just when Stella wanted something from her.

Stella came as close as nothing to hitting the dining room door for the second time in half an hour. She huffed and turned herself around, travelling past the empty secretary's desk outside the Director's office.

Stella turned right and then left and found herself in Rose Corridor. Rose residents were going through difficult times lately. Some residents from other corridors were calling them incontinent. As well, Rose had recently lost one of its own. Tildy had died the day before, and now her door stood half-open. Even without seeing inside, Stella knew that Ollie would have cleaned the place out already for the next occupant.

Stella heard a rattle and a thump inside Tildy's room. She took a step nearer and paused. What if Tildy had chosen to stick around after she died, as Mad Cassandra appeared to have done? What if Tildy was making the noise? But Tildy, in death as in life, was a Rose Corridor resident and had left this world angry at everybody at Fairmount except her nearest neighbours. Would she bother to haunt people she wasn't speaking to? Stella thought not. If there were a ghost here, using an empty room as a playground, let it be the ghost Stella sought. She stepped up to Tildy's door and opened it wide.

CHAPTER THREE

The grey morning light from Room 45's windows traced a silver outline around Mad Cassandra Browning's tangled salt-and-pepper hair, her narrow velveteen-jacketed shoulders, right down and around her skinny velour-covered legs. Even her knobbed bare feet with their yellow-horn toenails appeared magical in that silver gleam.

Stella said, "Cassie, please tell me, one way or another, are you dead or alive?"

"Dead on my feet," Cassandra snapped. "And alive with expectation. It's been a long time since you've come 'round to see me, Mrs Stella bloody Ryman."

Mad Cassandra reached out two bony hands and took hold of Stella's. There was no mistaking the cool touch of living skin against Stella's, nor the wiry strength behind the tug that propelled her into the room. Stella stumbled forward, her heart tumbling in her breast. The door, with a faint pneumatic whisper, closed behind her.

"Here." Backing away, Cassandra took hold of the visitor's chair by the bed and dragged it forward. "Stella Ryman, sit your heinie down here."

"Thank you, but I will sit on the bed," Stella said. "You take the chair. And while you're sitting there, I would like to ask you some questions."

"Oh, good." With an eager squeak of chrome legs against linoleum tile, Cassandra wiggled the visitor's chair towards the bed where Stella sat. She leaned towards Stella. Her eyes were alight with interest, and her breath was terrible. "Tell me, what's your latest case?"

"How did you know I have one?"

"You're always looking for something, Stella Ryman. What is it this time?"

"I'm looking for Thelma's fortune. Theo Longbourne said you were here ten years ago when Thelma arrived with a mah-jongg box full of money. Do you remember?"

"*Remember, remember, the fifth of November,*" Cassandra said. "Money, robbery, and boxes."

"I thought you might give me a straight answer, for once. It would be a nice thing to do for an old blind woman who's lost everything." Stella remembered that Cassandra had her own disabilities. Madness and death. Those were pretty serious handicaps. "I don't mean to be short with you, Cassie. But I wish you would help, because you're the only one I know who was here at the time Thelma arrived."

"Well, you've got that much wrong already, Stella Ryman."

"Have I?"

"Yes. Somebody else was here ten years ago."

"Who?"

"Thelma herself. What has she told you?"

Stella was silent.

"Stella, what have you asked Thelma?"

Stella realized that with all the talk of the mah-jongg box, she had not asked Thelma many details about her arrival there. The difficulties of time, age, and blindness had obfuscated that aspect of her detection process. "It's hard to get Thelma to talk."

"You're not in the detective business because it's easy, are you?"

Stella got to her feet. "No."

"Any more questions for me?"

"No. *Yes.*"

"Anything you like, you good old Stella."

"Cassie, why do you stay at Fairmount? When others leave, I mean?" Alice MacAndrew. Farley Lamoureux. And many more, including Tildy, in whose room the two stood face to face. "What is keeping you here?"

Cassandra laughed. "The same thing that's keeping you here, Stella. A taste for adventure. I'm like you. I make my own."

Stella remembered the *Choose Your Own Adventure* books she bought for her school library, long ago. She used to wonder why the kids liked them so much, flipping back and forth through the book instead of a good straight read-through. Now she knew: it was all about power over outcome. That was why they enjoyed them, and why Stella enjoyed being a detective.

Cassandra ducked out the door. Stella heard the dusty slap of bare feet outside in the corridor, moving away. She followed Cassie outside but found herself alone in an empty corridor. She rounded the corner and nearly collided with young Dr Terry and Reliza, the care worker with whom he was in love.

Stella looked from Reliza to Dr Terry. The two of them scowled at one another. She took a deep breath and said, "It's none of my business, of course, but I do think you two would be good for each other if you could just learn to get along."

Dr Terry cleared his throat and stuck his hands deeply into his pockets. Reliza shook her head wordlessly, patted Stella on the shoulder, and walked away.

Dr Terry sighed.

Stella said, "Go ahead and ask me something. I've asked you for advice often enough."

"Does doctor-patient confidentiality hold?"

"Naturally."

"Then can you tell me what is up with women?"

"Maybe. What happened?"

"I took her out for dinner. It was a nice place, and we had a good time. And now she won't look at me. What's going on, would you say?"

An incomplete patient history, Stella thought. She said, "Let me get a few facts."

She caught his wary look.

"Nothing too personal, Doctor, I promise. First, did you use the word *date*, as in *take you on a date*, when you asked her out?"

"I don't remember." He frowned. "*Date?* It's such a high school word that I doubt I would have used it. Still, there were candles and wine and all that jazz."

All that jazz. Stella wondered whether she ought to prepare him for her next question, rather the way a physician would warn a patient for the cold touch of the stethoscope. "When you said good night, were you by any chance a little over-romantic?"

"Certainly not. So, I ask you: what's wrong with Reliza?"

"Maybe nothing's wrong with her. Maybe it's all a misunderstanding. Maybe you should have kissed her."

Too late, she saw her error. His face slammed shut.

"You *did* kiss her. She wasn't ready. And then your feelings were hurt. Oh, for heaven's sake. Why can't two perfectly nice people just say they're sorry and move on?"

"Mrs Ryman, with all due respect, sorry doesn't mean a lot when you can't get a second date." Dr Terry kicked at an invisible stone on the corridor floor and walked off. Stella took the opposite path, and met Theo.

Some mornings she could wander the muddling corridors of Fairmount Manor for hours and never meet a soul, not even the ghost of Mad Cassandra. This was not one of those days.

"Hello, Theo," she said coolly.

He frowned. "I was looking for you."

"Well, you've found me."

Theo said, "It's about Thelma's money. I thought you might want to leave the building to search for it, and I have learned the new code for the front door keypad."

She frowned. "Why would the money be outside?"

"There's a garden shed back at the edge of the property."

"Wouldn't it be more likely that person would have spent it?"

"Yes. I'd imagine cold case files are the most difficult. At least on TV." He looked down at his shoes. "My wife watches a lot of *CSI*. Stella, I'm sorry I never mentioned my wife."

Stella blinked. She thought, *Reliza and Terry.* She said, "I'm sorry I made such a fuss about it."

They stood facing one another in the quiet corridor.

She said, "*CSI*? Well, that's not a bad show. But I prefer *Perry Mason*."

He smiled. "So do I."

Chapter Four

It was not yet lunchtime, but Stella found Thelma napping in her room. The shadows of leaves at the window waved like magic wands across the lump her tiny body made beneath the worn embroidered coverlet. Gold and red threads gleamed when the light touched them. It seemed a pity to wake her when she was so soundly asleep. But Stella remembered the line from many a thriller movie: *I'll sleep when I'm dead.* The import was as desperate and ironic in a care home as it was on an on-screen battlefield.

She whispered Thelma's name.

"I'm awake," Thelma muttered. "Is it an adventure?"

"Just a visit, I'm afraid."

"I'm pretty tired." Thelma struggled to sit up.

"Don't stir," Stella said. "I just want to ask you a few questions about the day you came to Fairmount."

"I walked to Fairmount."

Thelma had said so before, and Stella wondered how. She knew that Thelma had come here, still sharp, with failed eyesight, but how did she carry her belongings, including the mah-jongg box? "Did you live nearby?"

Thelma smiled. "I loved my house."

Long sold now. "What was your address?" Thelma told her an address on Larch Avenue, not far from Fairmount. A few streets away from Stella's old place. Stella knew Larch well. "We used to be neighbours, then."

"We're still neighbours," Thelma said. "Lower property values here, though."

Stella laughed. "I hated leaving home." She was not certain this was true when she left, but it was true now. "But the neighbours had all changed, strangers everywhere. Houses knocked down, new ones built. I suppose ..." this was difficult to admit. "... I was afraid to be on my own."

"My neighbours didn't change. The Lo family. Cindy was the little daughter." Thelma kneaded her coverlet with skinny fingers.

"Was she a good neighbour?"

"She was like my daughter. My granddaughter. Always underfoot, always making up stories. She used to sit up at night, writing them out in her bedroom when she was supposed to be asleep. Then she'd come next door and read them to me."

Startled at the thought of Thelma being actively fond of

another human being, Stella couldn't stop herself from asking, "Then why doesn't Cindy visit?" Too late, she thought, perhaps she didn't care. Or, perhaps she died.

Thelma said, "Cindy didn't want me to leave my home. She was angry with me and she wouldn't speak. She helped me carry my things on the back of her bicycle when I came to Fairmount, but she never said a word to me."

"And you've not seen her since?"

"No."

"You should have sent for her."

Thelma did not answer.

Stella asked the necessary question. "Were you afraid that she was the one who took your money?"

Thelma sat up straight in bed. Her face was creased in fury. "She didn't take the money. I offered to give it to her, and she wouldn't take it. Now, get out of my room."

"Sorry," Stella said. "You know that I had to ask."

Thelma fell back on her pillow. "I know. Get out."

Stella let herself out of Thelma's room. There was only one thing to do, and she would have to find Theo if she were to succeed at it.

CHAPTER FIVE

Stella stepped outside her own Room 34 at quarter past midnight. She stood poised in the half-lit corridor, straining to hear the crepe-soled care worker Serena walking her rounds about Fairmount. All was quiet.

Bedroom doors stood shut and dark in the dim. The only

open doorway was that of the staff room. It cast a white beam across the floor, and Stella would have to pass it somehow.

She crept along Daffodil Corridor, past the supply cupboard where last night she had hidden the *Hang in there, baby* cat poster. She moved towards the open staff room door and stopped to listen. A rush of water against metal told her that Serena was making herself a late-night potation, most likely Red Rose tea, as there was a huge box of it in the cupboard there. Stella had found out that much on an earlier investigation. This was not a very illuminating piece of information on its own, but the fact that the cupboard that held the box of tea was above and to the left of the sink, was. Serena had to lean forward to plug the kettle into the wall socket. And when she did, her view of the door would be blocked by the cupboard.

The rush of water stopped. Serena was plugging in. Stella smiled and slipped past the staff room door unseen.

Of course, there was the usual difficulty in finding the front door, and it wouldn't take Serena long to drink that cup of tea. Stella made her way as swiftly as she might in her excellent, silent lace-up shoes. Mad Cassandra had given Stella these shoes in the course of an earlier investigation, since the woman who had owned them before Stella had not needed them when she left Fairmount. She moved along the winding half-lit corridor, past more darkened bedroom doors and around the corner near the activities hall. She passed through Corridor Park and under the skylight, where rain pattered hard overhead. From there she achieved the front door. The three visitors' chairs stood facing Serena's empty cubicle with its light and phone. Stella read the keypad number off her wrist, where Theo had written it in ballpoint pen.

7744

All Stella had to do was punch it in.

She did not punch it in.

Blankness of mind comes to all, young and old, but Stella felt that she was getting an unfairly large share of the condition. This was worse than usual, because she was completely aware that she had a problem. Here was the front door. The keypad was on the wall to her left. Serena's cubicle, now empty, but who knew for how long, stood to her right. Stella knew that her goal was *outside*, and a few taps of her fingers on the keypad would get her there. But she couldn't think why she wanted to. Not tonight, with the rain pounding down.

A couple of weeks back, when she'd gone outside with Theo, the sky had been clear, and cherry blossoms glowed under street-lights. A magical moment, and anybody would desire to repeat it. Tonight, though, rain was falling, and the cherry trees would have dropped their blossoms by now.

So why was it so important to go outside that she was standing at the front door, risking capture and an end to all adventures should the Director find out? She looked again at her right wrist, where Theo had written the keypad number.

What about her other wrist?

She pushed back the left sleeve of her warm-up jacket and saw written there, in her own schoolteacher printing, the address of a house on Larch Street. And that did the trick. She remembered what she had forgotten.

A promise. One not lightly given, and certainly most seriously received.

One night very soon I'll knock on your door, and we'll do a silent midnight attack together.

Stella turned on her heel. With quick steps, and nearly directly, she made her way back through the corridors to wake Thelma and take her along on the night escape from Fairmount Manor.

CHAPTER SIX

Take one step, and take another. Let Thelma's cane clatter against the sidewalk and swipe at the laurels and other shrubbery in darkened gardens as the two adventurers walk by.

With Thelma setting the pace, their progress was agonizingly slow. *Soldier on, Stella.* At least the rain had stopped.

Stella said, "Is this the right way? It's been so long since either of us had to find Larch Avenue."

"Oh, it's easy as sin," Thelma said. "I'll bet you drove past Fairmount a hundred times on your way to work."

"I don't think I ever gave Fairmount a moment's thought, when I lived outside. Did you notice the place?"

"Like you notice a hole in the road," Thelma said. "But I found it in the end."

"Me, too." Stella didn't remember coming to Fairmount, but the Director, Mrs Perdita Warren, insisted that she had come on her own steam. The Warden had looked almost smug when she said that Stella had begged to be taken in.

Stella said, "Look, the last blossoms are falling from the cherry trees." Once she'd said it, she remembered once again that Thelma couldn't see them. She was sorry she'd made the same *faux pas* for the umpteenth time, but glad she'd brought Thelma along. She looked down. Even though the skies had cleared, the sidewalks were still wet, and Thelma's silk slippers made a soggy noise as she moved her feet slowly forward, one slipper after the other.

Stella tucked Thelma's arm more firmly under her own. "Tell me, how long did you live in your house on Larch?"

"Sixty years," Thelma said.

"I lived in my place for nearly that long. Funny, it doesn't seem like more than half a century."

"Speak for yourself."

Stella stifled her smile. "Were you born in the area?"

"I was born in China," Thelma said. "I came to this city to marry."

"I didn't know that," Stella said. "How long were you married?"

A silence followed. Stella remembered that she didn't like to talk about her own marriage and was about to make a tactful change of subject when Thelma spoke again.

"I came here when I was seventeen to marry a man who had seen a picture of me. It was a very fuzzy picture, because my family had paid well to have it unclear. My mother gave me her mah-jongg game, and my father changed a string of coins into twenty-five dollars to keep safely inside the mah-jongg box. He thought that the money might help to ease the gap between my photograph and my real appearance."

"There's nothing wrong with your appearance. Furthermore, if there's one thing I've learned, it's that every young woman is pretty in her way."

"Ha," Thelma said.

"It's true. And you are smart now, so you were smart then."

"Brains were not selling points in our day," Thelma said.

"How did the meeting go when you landed in America?"

"It went perfectly as far as I was concerned." Thelma swiped her cane through a blooming rhododendron. "I waited three hours on the dock with the stevedores walking round me and my luggage as if I were an unclaimed box of goods. Nobody met me. So I walked into town."

"How frightening." Stella attempted to imagine landing up in China alone, and failed.

"Not at all. I had those twenty-five dollars all to myself," Thelma said. "I got a job at a corner shop not far from here, and in the end, I bought the place and ran it for fifty years."

Stella nodded, lost for words. She wondered whether she might not have bought something at Thelma's corner store — apples or tea bags, perhaps. She peered ahead at the next street sign.

Thelma continued, "Even at the start, standing on the dock beside my suitcase, carrying my mother's black mah-jongg box, I knew the money inside it would be more use to me than a reluctant bridegroom. Money won't beat you, for a start."

Grimly, Stella said, "True."

"Money keeps you warm. If you're clever, it grows the way children grow, but it doesn't leave home. And it comforts you in old age."

"Does it?" Stella asked.

Thelma shrugged.

Stella said, "Isn't this Larch? That big house on the corner is new. I'm sure this street was all small houses with big gardens."

"Like mine," Thelma said.

Stella pictured a younger Thelma, skinny and wearing red. Walking without a cane. She imagined Cindy, the little girl who lived next door, walking at her side, making sure Thelma saw the curb all right, all the while chattering about the stories she stayed up late to write, even on school nights. *She was like my granddaughter.* If Cindy still lived next door to Thelma's old house, could Stella prevent herself asking the young woman why she had never come to Fairmount to see Thelma? Would the question not hurt Thelma more than Cindy? But Stella wanted to know.

Their arms linked, Stella and Thelma shuffled up Larch Avenue. Stella read the house numbers aloud, until Thelma said, "Stop."

Stella stopped. The rain was still holding off, but the sky was cloudy, so that the night bloomed up and around them like a dark blossom.

Thelma said, "Tell me about the middle three houses on this side."

Stella studied them. "The first appears to be quite new, with plate windows all darkened and a flat roof."

Thelma pinched Stella's arm. Stella winced, but understood that she was to continue. "The second is a pretty, older cottage, with one light on in the front room, and a lot of tulips springing up through the grass, dropping petals everywhere."

"Is there a Japanese maple?"

Stella peered at the second house's garden. The light in the front window was just enough to illuminate the red stars of the maple leaves by the front door. "Yes. And the third house is newer than the first. The garden hasn't been planted and the windows are taped."

"Never mind the third house. The first house is where the Lo family's should be, and the second house is mine."

Was. Stella said, "It's very pretty." Then she realized what the first house meant: the Lo family had moved away. She gazed from one house to the next and then up at the sky, while Thelma's crablike hand trembled at Stella's elbow.

"Yes, it's pretty. I meant what I said. I wish I had died here and never left it. Stella, let's go back."

"Are you sure?" Stella had brought Thelma on what she had promised would be an adventure. What kind of an adventure was it, if you came out to find a fortune and discovered only unattractive architecture and loss? Loss wasn't meant to deter a detective, nor ought it to halt an adventure. It was loss that sent a person on an adventure in the first place. From Homer to Tolkien, the search for something lost, whether personal or political, drove stories forward. It did not stop them short on page one and send them back to bed.

Stella studied the light in the front window of Thelma's old house. She didn't know whether she would have had the guts to do what she did next if the windows were darkened, as they were in most homes at this hour of the night. But in Thelma's house, somebody was sitting up late. Stella's early training was solid: one did not knock on anybody's door before nine in the morning or after nine at night. This was both.

"It's not too late to make this an adventure." Stella led Thelma up the short walk through the shadowed garden to the front door.

CHAPTER SEVEN

Stella was about to knock at the front door of Thelma's old home when Thelma reached into a shadow next to the door frame and pressed her forefinger on something there. A buzzing sound followed, loud against the night-time quiet. Then, following the doorbell's noise, nothing. Light from the living room shone, and Stella couldn't make out movement there.

Many people left lights on when they went out. Stella had sometimes wondered whether burglars didn't know that darkened houses meant people inside were asleep while houses still alight after midnight might mean their owners were away. What if she and Thelma became burglars now? How would they go about it? These old houses had narrow basement windows, but she couldn't imagine breaking one and rolling through it with Thelma to land on a concrete floor among boxes of apples and old clothing. Not at their age. A better way would be to find the back door with a window in it. Break the window, wrap her jacket around her arm to keep the glass from cutting her. Quick as a wink, they'd be in. That wasn't burglary, actually, because they wouldn't steal anything. They would only look around, so that would be breaking and entering.

The front door to Thelma's house opened.

A young woman stood before them. Stella looked past her. She saw a light upon a table in an otherwise shadowed living room. A chair stood nearby, facing an old sofa. A laptop computer sat open on the table.

Stella cleared her throat. "I'm Stella Ryman, and this is my friend —"

The woman said, "I know who she is."

Thelma gripped Stella's arm tightly. "Stella, is she Chinese?"

"Yes. Sorry, I mean Chinese Canadian."

Thelma said, "Hello, Cindy."

Cindy Lo took a step backward into the living room.

Stella led Thelma inside.

Cindy turned on the table lights in Thelma's old living room. The lamps lit the three women's feet more clearly than their faces. Cindy sat with her back to the table where she had been working at her laptop. Stella and Thelma were installed on an old sofa, which Thelma patted with one hand, the way Odysseus, Stella imagined, had patted his good old dog when he returned from years at war and at sea.

Cindy said, "You did come back. You said you would."

"I'm here," Thelma said.

Stella said, "I thought you lived next door."

Cindy gazed at her thoughtfully but didn't answer. She turned to Thelma. "Did you come back because they cured you?"

Thelma barked a laugh. "I forgot I told you that."

"You said they could stop you going blind."

"Nobody could stop it," Thelma said.

"She's not blind," Stella said. "She has macular degeneration."

"I'm blind," Thelma said.

"I'm sorry." Cindy looked down at her hands.

Stella broke the silence. "We came to see you, to ask you if you know what happened to Thelma's fortune that was in her Mah-Jongg box. She took it to Fairmount Manor Care Home and it disappeared."

Cindy frowned. "Yes, the care home. You told me it was a hospital, Thelma."

"Did I? I probably said that so you wouldn't visit. All those smells, it's no place for a child."

Stella knew that was not a good enough reason to keep a girl who was like your granddaughter from visiting. So why, then?

For the same reason I keep my daughter Junie at arms' length. I don't want her to see me like this. Diminished.

Stella gazed at Thelma. She saw a woman who had perhaps grown shorter over the past ten years, as had Stella herself. But in personality, in stature, and in courage, Thelma was not any smaller at all. She had not diminished. Stella would bet money that Thelma had become greater instead. Ten years at Fairmount could easily have killed her with boredom and loneliness, but instead it seemed to have made Thelma, if anything, bigger in spirit. Crankier, too, but that was just more of her natural self, like her tiny bones and taste for the colour red.

Stella said, "Where is Thelma's fortune? I know that you didn't take it, because Thelma says she offered the money to you and you refused."

Cindy said, "I took it."

Stella stared.

Cindy continued, "Thelma, I took it from your belongings when you went to the hospital. I mean the care home."

Thelma said nothing. She rested her hands one upon the other at the top of her cane.

Stella said, "Why?"

"Because I was only ten, and I thought you would come back home to get it. I knew you loved your money."

Thelma raised her gaze, met Cindy's, and they both smiled. Stella did not.

She asked again, "Where is Thelma's fortune?"

Cindy said, "Spent."

Stella tried to remember how many years a crime could be unreported and unsolved before the police could no longer investigate. Seven years? Fourteen? Or was that how long you had to wait to pronounce a person who had disappeared, dead? "How are you planning to give the money back?"

Cindy bit her lip and turned from Stella to Thelma. "At first I thought you would come home. I was a little girl who loved stories with happy endings, and I believed you when you said that your eyes would need treatment and you would come home. But you didn't come home. When my parents went to see you, they told me that you still didn't want me to visit."

"That doesn't answer my question," Stella said.

"It does. My parents—"

"Where are they?" Thelma asked.

"They sold our house and moved out to White Rock," Cindy said.

Stella said, "Please answer my question."

"Let her be, Stella Ryman," Thelma said. "I gave her the money. That's what I'll say to you and anybody who wants to know. So there."

"You did not give it to me," Cindy said. "I took the money out of the box and left it here in your house. It was easy, because you couldn't see. And when you didn't come back, I showed all that money to my parents. Hundred-dollar bills, lots of them. They said it was lucky your fortune was in cash and not the bank, because the institutions take most of an elderly person's money when they go into care."

Cindy looked at Stella, who nodded stiffly.

Cindy continued, "My parents said that you were tough and strong and you might change your mind and come out of the care home after all, and then what would you do? You couldn't live on the street. So, they used your money and some of theirs and they bought this house for you. They rented it out for a while, paid off the mortgage, and then I moved in." She looked at Stella with an apologetic grimace. "Being a writer doesn't pay very well."

"You grew up to be a writer?" Thelma said.

"You told me to, so what else could I do? Thelma, your room is here whenever you want to come home. I'll just move my things into your old office by the kitchen, and you can move back in."

Stella cleared her throat. "Cindy, I apologize."

"No, not at all. You are fierce and strong and that's what friends should be. I hope you will like me some day."

"I already like you," Stella said.

"I would already like you to make tea," Thelma added. "Nice and hot, please. My feet are all wet."

"I'll put your slippers on the radiator." Cindy removed Thelma's red slippers and took them out towards where the kitchen must have been.

On the sofa, Thelma settled back comfortably and closed her eyes. She looked so peaceful that Stella wondered for a terrible moment whether she had brought Thelma here to die at home, among friends, and sitting on her own sofa. It was not such a bad way to go, but Stella wasn't ready for Thelma to leave. Not even close to ready.

"Are you going to stay?" she asked. "Are you going to live here?"

Thelma tightened her hands on the cane top in her lap. "Not tonight. Cindy will drive us back once we've had some tea."

For the second time that night, Stella heard water running into a kettle, out in the kitchen. Cupboard doors opened and shut.

Stella said, "It's come to my attention that there are a number of mysteries needing solving at Fairmount. For example, where does the food money go? The cooks are always paying extra for us out of their pockets."

Thelma nodded. "I want to know what happened to the expensive mahogany tables that used to be in the dining room."

"And why does the Director arrive so late and leave so early?"

"Slow down a little," Thelma said. "Let's make the mysteries last."

"Let's," Stella agreed. "Do you believe that Cindy would cause a diversion tonight, so that we can sneak in past Serena and get back to our rooms undetected?"

"Piece of cake."

"Not alone." Stella leaned back and closed her eyes.

A clatter at the door told her the tea was ready. Stella decided that a cup of something warm was just the thing to drink when you were on an adventure. It would taste hot and wet in her mouth, like a kiss from the gods, and grant her strength and fortitude for all the adventures and mysteries that still lay ahead.

§

Mrs Stella Ryman's first five adventures can be found in the full-length novel Stella Ryman and the Fairmount Manor Mysteries. *The second collection of five novellas is due out in late 2018 from* Pulp Literature Press: *pulpliterature.com/stella-ryman-and-the-fairmount-manor-mysteries.*

STELLA RYMAN
AND THE FAIRMOUNT
MANOR MYSTERIES

MEL ANASTASIOU

ON A DARK LAKE'S EDGE

Angela Rebrec

Angela Rebrec is a writer, singer, and graphic artist whose work has appeared most recently in Prairie Fire, Grain, The Antigonish Review *and* EVENT. *Her writing has been shortlisted for* PRISM International's *Creative Nonfiction Contest and this piece was shortlisted for* Pulp Literature's Magpie Award. *As well, she facilitates weekly writing workshops with elementary-school-aged children. Angela lives with her husband and three children in Delta on unceeded Coast Salish lands.*

On a Dark Lake's Edge

Amelia draws patterns in the scree with a whittled branch. Lines emerge as the wood flexes under her touch. She sings something familiar, though she claims it all her own. Bryan has taken the older ones on a night-hike in search of bugs — the missing flashlights.

> spruce flank the campsite
> an afternoon's joyful dance
> what size this rainbow?

The tree-line lost in the twilight. As I whittle more sticks for marshmallows, Amelia and Steven cocoon under a fleece blanket. Another log goes on the fire. *Remember how Raven tricked Seagull into releasing the sun?* The children caw in response. The spruce lean-in a little closer.

> Raven's night-jacket
> he wears as a reminder —
> he will trick you too

Earth will not disclose her age: all the stories we have told since the beginning. The fire ebbs as we carry our children to their sleeping bags. These taiga nights burn like glacial-fed lakes.

> night sky
> takes flight —
> Apus, Aquila, Cygnus

Everything grows stunted: lodgepole pine, salal, labrador tea. Jason recalls how his sister's young neighbour was hit by lightning. All the wailing at the funeral. Dark whiskey keeps us warm. A picture grows in my chest, cross-hatched and shaded. Our tents grow taller as the fire smoulders.

> midnight ablaze with sound
> hush
> children sleep

THE BRIGHTNESS OF THINGS

Jessica Barksdale

Jessica Barksdale's fourteenth novel, The Burning Hour, *was published by Urban Farmhouse Press in April 2016. Her novels include* Her Daughter's Eyes, The Matter of Grace, *and* When You Believe. *A Pushcart Prize, Million Writers Award, and Best-of-the-Net nominee, her short stories, poems, and essays have appeared in or are forthcoming in the* Waccamaw Journal, Salt Hill Journal, Little Patuxent Review, Carve Magazine, Palaver, *and* So to Speak. *She is a Professor of English at Diablo Valley College in Pleasant Hill, California, and teaches novel writing online for UCLA Extension. She holds an MA in English Literature from San Francisco State University and an MFA from the Rainier Writers Workshop at Pacific Lutheran University. You can read more at jessicabarksdaleinclan.com*

THE BRIGHTNESS OF THINGS

"**Maxine Whitshaw?**" the man on the phone said after Max's hello.

"Yes?" Max clenched her cell phone between her collarbone and the tip of her chin. At that moment, she was on a step stool, looking for her father's baton. The back of the cupboard over the fridge was a place no one ever put anything, so she'd waited to search here till nothing else offered up the stick. Of course, there it had been, hiding at the back.

"My name is Davis Smith, and I'm calling from Precise Aeronautics."

Her phone in one hand, the baton in the other, she backed off the stool, staring at the stainless steel door of the enormous fridge her husband Ronnie had insisted on during the remodel. With three children under ten, thirty fingers between them, the front was a collage of smudgy handprints with milk, peanut butter, and strawberry jam embellishments.

Davis Smith waited on the line. Max tried to think why anyone from any aeronautic company would call her.

"Huh?" She put the baton on the granite counter top and pulled the phone away from her face, looking at the number. A strange area code. Richmond, Virginia.

"You entered the lottery —"

Max shook her head, snorted. Phone spam. Telemarketers. Desperate people making money desperately. She hung up and slid the phone into her dress pocket. Picking up the baton, she twirled it a bit, remembering her father using it with much more gravitas. In front of an orchestra, raising it in his hand, the room silent. And then down with a flourish. Waaah — the sounds of every instrument filling the air. Her mother sitting still next to her, rapt as they both stared at Max's father's sleek black hair.

Max's phone buzzed, and she pressed the button to silence it. After she gave her eldest child, Hazel, the baton (a potential prop for the school spring play), she'd get online and re-up her number for the no-call list.

But later, sitting at the computer, her phone buzzed again. And again, it was Davis Smith.

"Don't hang up. I'm serious."

"About what?" Max asked.

"About the lottery. No one believes me the first time. Mostly, it takes me four calls. I've resorted to texts."

Max paused, clicked on the no-call list's 'submit'. The form zinged into the ether, she sat back in her chair and waited for Davis to finish. After she got rid of him, she was free and clear for what? Three years? She must have not re-upped when she was supposed to.

"Candygram," she said. "Might work."

"Candygram?" Davis asked. She imagined him writing down the suggestion.

"Stripper," Max went on, sitting back in her computer chair. "Stripper singing telegram. Vienna Boys Choir. Something big, Davis."

"This is big, Maxine."

At the bottom of her computer, her email notification popped up. A message from Precise Aeronautics. Lottery winner, it read. Space Shuttle.

"Who are you?" Max asked, leaning toward her computer, her elbows resting on the wood. Pages she should have been editing crinkled under her forearms.

Precise.

"I told you. I'm calling from Precise Aeronautics." Davis was weary. "I'm calling to let you know you won the trip."

"The trip."

"To the moon."

"I won a trip to the moon," Max said flatly, but something flashed in her memory. Something on a website. A travel site. In order to join, she had to enter to win. She must have. All she'd really wanted to do was look at the photos of Portugal and Tanzania. The ocean. A safari. Anything but read other people's bad writing. So she'd given out her email and her phone number. And voilà! Davis called. Not that Precise would really send her. How could they? There would be regulations and things that she would fail. Probably the weight requirement (of course, perhaps one weighed less on the moon. Or was it more? In space, she'd be light as air). But here? On an Earth scale? She'd be done. Over. A goner. Total failure, as with so many endeavours. Just last night. That tomato sauce. And the baton? Hazel had wanted it this morning. Hadn't Max needed to rush it to the school about fifteen minutes ago? Wasn't the audition going on right now without a proper conductor's baton?

"Look, I know this seems crazy. But our founder wants to make Precise Aeronautics moon missions accessible. For the people."

"Mostly rich people," Max said. She knew about Rupert Forsythe. Wacky, wild, crazy British loopster who already owned everything and was now expanding his empire off-world. His dyed blond wig-like mop. His crazy black eyebrows. A hip Groucho Marx.

"We are scheduling our first four flights. We estimate the first in five months. August fifteenth, to be precise. You will be on our third voyage."

"I won," Max said.

"I'll say," Davis said. Max could almost hear him wipe his brow. "Just think. One-point-four million people filled out the entry form. And you? One of four winners! Maxine, it's a miracle."

It turned out that not being on the first voyage was the miracle. Crash landing, no survivors. Not even that flight's lottery winner. Forsythe went back to the drawing board.

"We will have to postpone your take-off," Davis told her on one of his monthly calls. She'd filled out all the forms (liability, for one, clearly necessary), gone to the doctor (her weight was just fine), completed all the blood work and scans, taken the shots, and started a diet and exercise regime. In the coming months, she would head off to space camp to learn about anti-gravity and dehydrated food. All that was left was to tell her family.

"Not surprising." Max sat at her desk, the computer screen open to a memoir about growing up in a cage. When she received the manuscript, Max wondered if she'd survive the reading, the author's life a harrowing experience of survival. But the prose ached for verbs and detail. *Confined, trapped, tortured, stuck* were strangely absent from the long narrative.

"You aren't a writer," the managing editor had told her once. "You're a copy editor. So stop suggesting stuff you shouldn't. Your bailiwick? Commas. Semicolons. Anachronisms. Number format. Come on, Max!"

"It's all been figured out," Davis told her. "Really. It had something to do with batteries. Simple."

"How many people died?"

Davis was silent for a moment. "I know. But you don't have to worry. Your family doesn't have to worry."

Max imagined that her husband Ronnie would not be worried. At all. In fact, he'd probably pack her moon case.

"Just let me know if it's going to be real," Max said. "You know, people do have lives. Going to the moon takes some time out of the schedule. People have responsibilities."

"Do they?" Davis said, his voice heavy with too many phone calls.

"You're right. Probably not. But let me know, okay?"

"Will do." Davis hung up.

"Who was that?" Hazel asked. Max turned towards her office door. Her daughter stood there clutching her school backpack. She looked exactly as Max had as a child, except pretty. Dark hair, dark eyes, slight and small. But there was a sweet softness about the eyes and lips. That was Ronnie. And the boys were him exactly, no evidence of Max in their long bones, bright faces, thick dark blond hair. Even though John and Ryan were only five and seven, everyone always noted they'd be 'lady killers'.

What a thing to say.

Max formed her lie. "A man who has a job for me. But it keeps not happening."

Hazel nodded. She understood about the vagaries of editing. The influx of work and then the spaces of nothing in Max's life.

Ronnie, on the other hand, was a constant working machine. Up at 5:30 am, home at 7:00 pm. Golf (or so he said) on one or two weekend afternoons.

"Clients," he had said when she first complained about having to drive the children to every activity and party and soccer match by herself. "You know the game."

Max did know the game, and she hadn't been thinking about investment banking.

"When will the job happen?" Hazel asked as they walked down the hall toward the kitchen. John and Ryan still had another hour to sleep before Max had to wake them up. At nine years old, Hazel took the early bus, finally free from her brothers' questions and demands.

"In a blue moon," Max wanted to say but didn't. "When the cows jump."

She didn't say that either.

"Soon, I hope," Max said. "But don't worry. I'll tell you when it happens."

When Hazel sat at the table, she turned to rummage through her backpack. "Here," she said, holding out the baton. Max had made it to the final performance, the baton becoming Hazel's witch wand.

Max took it, the wood smooth under her hand. She could almost feel the old music.

"I've arranged everything," Max said, her duffel bag packed and by the front door.

"You're shitting me, right?" Ronnie stood in front of the fireplace. "You think you're going to the moon?"

"I am going to the moon," Max said.

"What about the kids?"

"I told them already. Precise has a live feed they can watch from the computer. There's a kind of Skype thing. I showed Hazel—"

"Shit!" Ronnie stomped around, pushing one hand through his blond but greying hair. When they'd met in college, it had shone white. He'd been a Nordic dream-god-man to Max's flirty, gamin, fake self-image. For a while, it had worked.

"They crashed the first time!" Ronnie shouted. "What am I supposed to do if that happens?"

"Shhh." Max stood, glossing over the whole topic. "Stop it. Yes, they crashed. But not the second time. Things went perfectly."

"Did you see them up there?" Ronnie waved his hands skyward. "In that moon house. What is that guy thinking? British nutjob, that's what he is. God. Yes, that's it! He thinks he's God!"

Max picked up her duffel bag. The children were in bed. Betsy, the nanny, was coming at six the next morning, just before Ronnie left for work. Max had showed the children her photo online, a middle-aged woman with short gray hair and kind brown eyes.

In preparation, Max had posted a detailed schedule for the two weeks she'd be gone: school, classes, and parties. There were meals stacked like flat shiny astronauts in the freezer. Lasagne, mac and cheese, meatballs, vegetable soup. Betsy would have Max's car and sleep in the guest room. Precise was picking up the cost.

"You're really going to the moon, Mommy?" John had asked, his blue eyes wide as the Earth she would soon be looking down upon. Innocent, for now.

"I am, sweetie."

"Can I come?"

By the time John was an adult, people like Forsythe would be running daily shuttles to the moon and the moon spas. Maybe even Mars. After all, NASA had just made it to Pluto. In a few years, Ronnie could golf on the scorched, oxygen-empty ground under a bubble. Maybe his game would improve.

Max put her hand on the doorknob. Outside, a cab was waiting. "Look, you know you're only upset that the schedule is rattled. Bottom line, it's a relief. A break. Right?"

Ronnie stilled, watched her, his wide eyes John's.

"I'll be back in two weeks. A little less," Max said, opening the door and stepping out onto the porch, the moonlight — no, it was streetlight — all around her.

Since all the space shuttle incidents and NASA's folding up of manned inter-moon and planetary missions, Max hadn't bothered to keep up with the latest developments. Actually, she never really had. But she'd watched the news, seen the rockets go up and the shuttles hurtle down. She'd seen them blow up a couple of times, shards and chunks tumbling towards the earth, black and smoking. The spectators pressing hands against agonized mouths, disbelief and then horror in their eyes.

But now things had changed. The shuttle was like a small powerful jet, beefy and thick, nose and body like a squat but powerful porpoise.

"Can it actually lift off?" a man next to her asked. He'd been on the chartered plane she'd boarded at LAX. Now they were in the California desert, the exact location a secret.

"Enough so that it can crash," another man answered. "Jack."

He held out his hand first to the other man (Mario) and then to Max.

They were sitting in a waiting area, bags at their feet, looking out a window at a group of six other people walking down the tarmac past the shining, stubby shuttle towards the building in which they all sat. Max realized she was only one of two women. Two among seven. Something pinged in her. An alert. A siren. A *siren*.

Max introduced herself, her heart beating in her throat. She was going to the moon. With these people. Strangers. It was like the first day of school.

The door whooshed open, pulling in hot air. From another door, the instructor who had greeted Max initially and two other similarly-garbed people (one a woman) came in, carrying bags and clipboards. The room filled with noise, the stilted loudness of the first hour of an awkward cocktail party.

The woman walked around handing out the bags — which were actually backpacks — and one of the men passed out the clipboards. The first man — Marshall — stood at the front of the room and called for everyone's attention.

"Thank you all for getting here on schedule. I know how hard that can be with other airlines," Marshall said, giving the group a wink. There were polite laughs. "But this won't be like any other airline that you've been on. After some training, you will be going to a place no one else flies to. Can't fly to. And no one but Precise has a groundbreaking, state-of-the-art moon unit."

Marshall looked around the room, wide-eyed and waiting, but whatever he was waiting for didn't happen.

"He must have named it 'moon unit,'" Jack whispered into Max's ear. "Wants a pat on the back."

Max turned a little to take in Jack. He smelled clean and rich, all the fibres on his body brand-spanking new. His underwear was probably never worn and the highest quality. He probably didn't even buy it himself, Max thought. His wife. His butler. His maid. His housekeeper. Or, at least, Amazon. His hair was a rich dark brown, a cap on his perfectly featured head. He was what? Thirty? A specimen from the permanently rich, a lucky fellow whose college degree was just trimming.

She was only thirty-five, permanently middle-class, and mostly educated, but she knew where the name of their moon abode came from. She just didn't have the energy to explain that the musician Frank Zappa named his daughter exactly that: Moon Unit.

Jack smiled when he noticed her gaze. His skin was like lightly browned butter. Obviously, he was not one of the lottery winners. No, Jack, with his new clothes, shiny leather shoes, and perfect skin paid 1.2 million for his moon vacation.

"For these first few days, however," Marshall continued, "you will be training on our space shuttle, *The Vivant.*"

Marshall turned towards the window, motioning with one sweeping arm at the shuttle they'd all been staring at anyway.

Everyone clapped, as if forgetting, Max thought, the nine people who died on the other shuttle. What was it called? As she clapped, she racked her brain. Oh, yeah. *The Gift.*

That keeps giving.

"So please follow Charlotte into the barracks. It's unisex. Just like everything. Bathrooms included. The future is here at Precise."

Max clomped behind the crowd, her backpack swinging on her arm. She looked at the clipboard and the list of names as they walked out of the building and across the tarmac: Jack, Anne, Steve, Thom, Mario, Bruce, Jorge, Xavier, Maxine. Just like in school. Off to learn something but at the back, the end, as usual.

Except, she was very good at moving around in the anti-gravity simulator, a large Quonset hut of joy on the edge of the training facility. She'd been a good swimmer and had even been on the diving team one year. Her back still arched. Her feet flexed. Bouncing was her specialty. But in her space suit and alone in air, every muscle moved in concert.

"You're a mermaid!" Anne said.

Maxine turned round and round, one knee bent, pushing herself as she indeed had under water.

"Quite a spinner," Jack said as he sailed by. Jorge gave her a dark glance as she spun away from her own air circle. He was "Whore-Hey." At least, that's how she remembered to say his name. He zipped past her. Even without gravity, she could smell his aftershave, the kind that only a CIA operative could wear. Amber and ice.

Steve, Thom, Mario, and Xavier looked like arctic boy scouts in their white belted suits, all of them clumped together at one end of the simulator. They grabbed at each other, spun around, laughing, flinging each other in ever-widening arcs. It was hard to believe they were, in order, a state senator, a social media company mega-millionaire, a tennis champion, and a movie star-slash-icon.

Only Bruce — corporate lawyer — seemed allergic to weightlessness, thundering and bumping around the tube like a broken bumblebee. "Uh," he moaned. "Uh."

The rest of them? A *corps de ballet*.

They slept for three nights in the barracks. They were heavy in their beds, back on Earth for another twelve hours. Anne spun under her stiff blankets, the sound a crackling ratchet amongst the male complement of snores. A best-selling advice columnist, Anne was more used to the Ritz and Four Seasons than boot camp bed rolls.

"I just want to get the hell out of here," she whispered. The barracks may have been co-ed, but Max and Anne had segregated themselves at the far wall.

"Aren't you scared we'll crash?" Max asked. This after a panicked Skype with Ronnie and the children. She hadn't shown it, answering their questions, showing off her fancy suit. But after the call ended, the shaking started, every system—those very ones she learned about in high school physiology—heaved in her body as if trying to escape. How dare she try to take them off planet!

"There are worse ways," Anne said. And she would know. All those emails. All those letters. All that pain. "Anyway, the last one made it."

"Two days is a long time on the moon," Max whispered.

"It's a long time anywhere," Anne said.

"What are we going to do there?" Max asked. "Play cards? Charades? Write? Watch Netflix?"

Anne was silent, and for a second, Max thought she was crying. The terror had finally caught up with her, all her advice run out, even for herself. But the herky sound under the terrible blankets wasn't crying. It was laughter, the sound Max finally fell asleep to.

After the fear that they would die on lift-off passed, the shuttle takeoff seemed almost normal. If she hadn't been looking out the window, Max might have thought she was on the United Airlines Flight 930 to London, a red-eye, only 36,000 feet above the earth, speeding over Greenland. *The Vivant,* under her seated body, whirred and chugged, the noise deafening even with earplugs and a helmet. She felt the G-forces press her against the seat, but the pressure was like a large hand, constantly but patiently subduing her. It was like a constant takeoff, a flight manned by a novice pilot, hard and jerky but not death-defying.

And she was looking out the window, her face pressed against the quadruple-paned but tiny glass porthole. She was hurtling up past that whisk of white, oxygen, the atmosphere, the earth below a swirling orb of blue and enormous cloud, just like in the posters.

You are here. A red arrow pointed to the planet.

But she wasn't there. Not anymore. Not after the flare of sparks and heat as they passed through the thing that made them earthlings, the technology Forsythe paid billions for. Pop, and they were space creatures. Pop, and Max was untethered. Free.

As per the lecture at space camp, there was a surge. A rocket firing from the back of the shuttle, and then they were propelled towards the moon, fuelled by an ion drive, whatever that really was. For the next three days — Marshall had outlined the trajectory on the PowerPoint — they would complete the 384-kilometre journey, achieve lunar orbit, and then land, a process that involved a portion of the shuttle detaching like an escape pod from any number of sci-fi movies. From the pod landing site, they would be picked up by the moon shuttle and taken to the moon unit, where they would stay for two nights, though Max questioned the notion of night on the moon. Dark side, bright side? Where would they be in relation to the sun? Or the earth, for that matter? Obviously, she hadn't been paying much attention. She decided to not worry about it because at this point, strung up in the deep dark space speckled with pinpricks of light and stars, there was very little she could do about anything.

Also, as soon as the seat belt sign was turned off (yes, really) and the cabin attendant went to check on the pilot and crew, Max understood what Anne's plan for the next few days entailed.

The rustling sounds came from Anne's sleeping cubicle. Then that laughter. Clearly, she and Xavier (missing from the cabin) had taken off their helmets and suits, using the convenient openings in their compression skin suits to free important body parts for the activity at hand.

"What kind of club is this? The ten-thousand-mile-high club?" Bruce asked as he bumped by, floating, sort of, as he grabbed from chair back to chair back. He wasn't that heavy, Max thought. But he was resisting buoyancy, urging himself to ground even when there wasn't any ground.

Max almost asked him what he meant, but then remembered sex in airplane bathrooms occurring at a high cruising altitude. She and Ronnie had never had sex on an airplane, not even a grounded one. Or really any place other than a bed, usually their bed. Hazel had already been on board when they got married, so they had rarely travelled together, save for those few months before Hazel's birth. But from the moment of her daughter's conception, Max had been queasy and wan, preferring to stay home rather than accompany Ronnie on his regular trips to

New York and London, places they'd enjoyed. Before marriage. Before children. Before they stopped wanting to be together.

Anne's low, guttural laugh had no gravity, filling the shuttle from floor to ceiling, though, of course, it was hard to know which was which at this point.

Bucket list, Max thought. Have sex in space.

Bucket list. Have sex on the moon.

Max floated to the observation platform, which was a stretch of the term, the space only as big as a normal rear airplane galley, but unlike the rest of the craft it had two larger windows. Jack bobbed in front of one, staring down at the earth, taking photos with his phone. He turned when he noticed Max.

"Fancy a drink?"

Jack wasn't British, so Max questioned the 'fancy'. Also, she questioned drinking, though the spacecraft attendant had shown them the self-serve liquor vault as they boarded. "Isn't one in space like ten on the ground?"

"We're drunk without even having started." Jack flipped the latch and switch for the vault. "Grey Goose?"

Despite the alcohol, it wasn't Jack that was first. One tiny Grey Goose, and Max floated to the back of the shuttle, her eyes shut, the empty bottle clutched in her hand. She woke with Mario next to her, both of them wedged in his sleeping pod. His hands ran up and down her compression suited body, hers on his. And wow! Even covered with tight material, Mario was a star, the tennis victories written all over each muscle. His body radiated like a pulsar, his heartbeat a slow one-two even as he panted in her drunken ear.

As she moaned into pleasure, she wished she were just a bit more conscious. She wanted to remember her infidelity, at least enough to feel super guilty about it later. There was more panting and some groaning, and then nothing but space all around them.

In the hours before entering the moon's orbit, there was Thom. She'd read a lot about him — hard not to when she spent a portion of every day on his company's social media site — and though she'd never really imagined all this pre-moon sex, she would have assumed the billionaire would be the one having it. Because he could.

But he was quiet in bed, pulling Max on top, their suits grinding away together. This time she was sober, and as he closed his eyes, grimacing in pleasure — or what substituted for it — Max watched him, her body going on without her thoughts. She'd gotten past the guilt and shame of infidelity after Mario (things seemed to happen faster in space) so she wondered, as Thom pushed inside her, how he had been the one to make all that money. What choices had he made that she had not? And yet, here they were, together, in space. Sure, she'd won her trip. Sure, she was just a part-time copy editor with three children living in the suburbs. In a failing marriage, or at least a disentangling one. But now? Here? She and Thom Buckingham were even.

They woke to the voice of the pilot, telling them to return to their seats.

"Man," said Thom, his blue-green gaze on hers. How many times had she seen this face? None, really. Only once in real life, here on this trip. Not that this trip was real.

"Yeah," Max said, and they floated out of the pod and clambered into their space suits and helmets, allowing the attendant to assist them. Back in their seats, all of them strapped in and locked down, the orbit and landing protocols began.

Xavier said, "One small step for man ... " And then seemed to forget the rest. Next there were thrusters and trajectories. The cabin detached, and they plunged down, stars, space, and Max's whole life flashing past her little window.

What was Hazel doing right now? Was she laughing? Were the boys in their bath? Had they eaten their broccoli at dinner? Was Ronnie coming home at night? Did he read them stories?

Something seemed to yank them up, Max's breath jumping to the roof of her mouth. And then they settled, settled, settled, and clanged down. She opened her eyes, not realizing she'd jammed them shut and tight. Turning toward the window, she saw the white, pocked, pillowy surface of the moon.

"What's all that damn mess out there?" Steve asked, his voice Southern and raspy. She hadn't slept with him, yet. Maybe Anne had. All his fundamentalist preaching might be just a vote show.

"Space garbage. Leftover landing junk."

"Maybe you should lobby for a recycling program, Steve," Thom said.

In her headset, Max heard people sniggering. Thom was a notorious environmentalist. At least online. In reality, he had torn down an entire San Francisco block of historical houses and gardens to build his new twelve-thousand-square-foot mansion that he shared with his neurosurgeon wife.

The attendant was up, releasing the seat locks, helping them out of their bindings. There was a clunk at the door. They all walked toward the back, carrying the few belongings they were allowed. In her spacesuit, Max felt like the Pillsbury Doughboy. With her helmet, a goldfish. And yet, she kept hearing HAL's voice saying, "I'm sorry, Dave. I'm afraid I can't do that."

But the moon shuttle's door stayed open, and they all filed

in, the attendants closing the doors, leaving the cabin behind at the moon landing site. Then they bounced off, heading to the moon unit. Climate controlled, gravity at almost normal ("You'll feel like you've had a cleanse," Marshall had said. "At least five pounds lighter!"), the moon unit would attempt to replicate the atmosphere on earth. They'd be back on ground, using their own bones and muscles to keep upright.

As she peered through the window, Max watched the shuttle bound and surge over the moon, past mounds of more junk, dipping down into a valley where she soon saw a building in the distance. At first, it seemed like an assortment of igloos, but as the shuttle barrelled ever forward, she noted that each igloo was interconnected by tubes. As they rounded the first igloo, she saw there was a giant igloo in the centre, all tubes leading toward the centre. Out the other side of the shuttle, she noted a farm of solar panels, all gleaming silver in the harsh sunlight.

After a few moments, the shuttle slowed and another docking procedure ensued. Air hissed. Parts clanged together. A lurch. A stop. A lurch. A stop. She could almost hear HAL. "Just what do you think you are doing, Dave?"

Then the attendants were up, freeing them from yet another set of restraints. Silently, in a row, they all walked toward the exit. At the rear, Max counted how many people she hadn't slept with.

As if checking into a Four Seasons room with a personal concierge, and once they'd taken off their spacesuits and hung them in a 'coat room' near the entrance, they were led individually to their own private igloo. Or piece of an igloo.

"You're going to love it up here," the young man said. He was dressed as though this were a Carnival Cruise. Nautical epaulets on his shoulders (gold and black). A white short-sleeved shirt, white pants, soft velvety white shoes. "Forsythe has made the moon accessible."

Some tag line, she thought, almost laughing. But then she realized it likely *was* the tag line.

After a tour of the accommodations, the young man in white left, the doors whooshing behind him. Max stared out her oval window, blinking into the glare of the moon, darkness hovering over the white.. She dug through her bag to find the device Precise had given them, an iPad on steroids.

She clicked, and in what felt like longer (and how could it not be longer?), Ronnie's face was on her screen. He smiled, the screen wavered, stilled, and then he was back.

"Are you there?"

She nodded, unable to say a word. Instead, she picked up the device and walked it over to the window. Max heard Ronnie call for the kids, and then as she held the screen out toward the moon and the vast black of nothingness all around her, she heard their sounds of awe. What other sounds were possible?

After a minute, she gave them the same tour of her pod that she'd been given. More sounds of awe. But then she had to look at them, all three kids in front, their smiles, two gap-toothed, one not. But all beaming. Ronnie, in the back, smiling at her in a way he hadn't for years. All of them were wide-eyed, open-mouthed as if breathless, staring at her as if she'd done more than just enter a lottery.

She had to hang up, so she did, telling them she had to get to dinner. But what she did instead was lie back on the large but very hard bed and fall asleep.

Everyone was assembled at the large table, including Forsythe himself, who must have stayed on after the last flight. The artificial light that filled the room shone on his full head of over-dyed blond hair that stuck up straight and seemed held to his head like a hat. His teeth were as white as the moon, and as he talked he waved one hand like a dancer. Or a conductor, his movements punctuating every sentence. Every word, even.

Davis was young and lean, tight and trim like the young man who'd shown Max to her room. In fact, all the men seemed that way. When introduced to Max, he beamed, teeth as white as his boss's.

Attendants buzzed around the table, putting down plates filled with food that must have arrived on the latest shuttle. Bowls of vegetables, plates of sliced meats. Potatoes and rice and pasta. Max sat back in her chair, watching them all. Even off earth, they had more than the 9 9 percent. They were sitting on a rock with no air or water but living like they had them anyway.

The attendants made a show of popping corks, and Bruce whispered in her ear, "One on the moon is like twenty on Earth."

When everyone had been served, Forsythe raised his glass. "To those of you who made —"

Bruce whispered, "Survived."

" — the trip," Forsythe continued, "may this adventure be the first of many and lead to a new colony for humankind."

"Bet you're glad he said *human* and not *man*." Bruce bent over his glass, hiding his laughter. Clearly he was headed toward that twenty on Earth.

They all clinked glasses and started eating, Max finally hungry. She'd barely eaten on the shuttle ride, certain at first that she would die and then a little too busy to take much time out for a snack. Now, it was as if she was starving.

"One pound on the moon is twenty on Earth," Bruce hiccupped, pouring himself another glass.

Across the table, Xavier was leaning toward Anne, whispering in her ear. Anne's gaze bore into Max, so she turned her gaze to Thom, who was leaning into Mario. (That was a development.) Jorge was taking considered and thorough glances at them all, in order. She wasn't sure, but he seemed to be talking to himself — or into a recorder. Forsythe, the man of the hour and *Time* magazine's Man of the Year, had a long rich arm around Davis while listening to Steve expound on illegal moon immigration. Everyone else just drank. Except Jack, who, like Anne, was staring at Max. She smiled back at him. He raised his glass.

Later, over a 'pudding', Forsythe walked the table, stopping to chat with each and every guest. He'd not buttoned his top shirt button, showing off his compression suit neckline. A real space cowboy.

"So are you liking your journey with us, Mrs Whitshaw?"

Max nodded. "Max, please. Thank you so much for the opportunity. It's amazing."

"A small word for all this," Forsythe said, his hand moving again to the inner music that accompanied him. "Opportunity, that is."

"Well, I mean, privilege, I guess."

He smiled, beatific and lofty. "You're a lovely part of our puzzle."

Max sat up a bit, almost reaching out to grab him so he'd explain the word puzzle (no hand gesture with that), but Davis walked over, whispered in his ear, and Forsythe cleared his throat.

"I'm needed at control, my dear guests. I'll see you tomorrow in the atrium. Please don't hesitate to ask the staff for your every need."

Max remembered a line from *Jurassic Park*: "'We spared no expense.'"

That hadn't gone as planned, had it?

Then Davis whisked him away. Max sat back, looked at all these people, all of them powerful. But it would only take one solar wind or an alien blast or a surge of cosmic junk and they wouldn't be running from velociraptors but Sandra Bullock in *Gravity* without George Clooney to save them. No, they'd float away, cracking into shards of ice. Gone. All this money, all this power. Poof!

"Why do you think I won the lottery?" she asked Jack later as he sat on the edge of her bed, pulling on his nifty space station pyjamas.

Jack shrugged, a classic good boy shrug, the kind he'd learned growing up in Manhattan and the Hamptons. At Phillips Exeter Academy and then Harvard. And now, at his family's investment firm, where he really didn't need to work, the family fortune built on the backs of all the people who ever earned a dollar in the United States.

"He said I was part of a puzzle."

Jack laughed, stood. "Aren't we all?"

"Even here?"

"More here."

"Well, it won't last."

Jack turned and looked at her, hands on his perfect hips. "Nothing does. Soon enough, we'll be home. The moon will just be the moon again."

But wasn't the moon supposed to be the moon, Max wondered? Wasn't home home?

The lack of gravity got to everyone. Standing, but not. Blood circulating, but more slowly. Up sometimes seemed down. Arms moved in ways that seemed a surprise. Max studied Steve's hand for a time, thinking it was hers. Organ failure would be in the cards for anyone staying too long. Forsythe seemed to be floating. Around the bright atrium, his laughter was like the clouds that were painted on the domed ceiling. In the corners, the guests were acting out a Roman orgy, feasting and kissing and walking off to their rooms in various couplings. Max felt her brain, at least most of it, cease working. Beyond any jetlag she'd ever experienced, she felt drugged and wondered if this were all just some bad LSD trip. In Jorge's or Anne's arms (wow, check that off the list), she found it hard to keep track of her own movements, her pleasure like the soundtrack from a TV show on in a faraway room.

Back in the dining area for their last meal, she finally saw it. The puzzle that she was a part of. Forsythe waved his hands, moving them all the way he wanted to. The true father of the mission, he'd put this person and that person and all the people at the table. They acted to his whim, this multi-billion dollar extravaganza, a Versailles in the middle of the moon's desolation. Rome could burn and they would never feel it. As long as there were ions to fuel the shuttle and solar panels and exercise bikes, Forsythe might not ever have to go home and be among non-Forsythe-organized humans again.

"Good night," someone whispered to her later. A voice near her ear. Bruce? Steve? But the voice was familiar, old, known. She reached out to grab him—it was a him—but by the time her hand was out and searching, she was asleep.

In her seat, strapped down and encased in her suit, Max watched the pockmarked surface of the moon smooth in the distance, shining bright. Her heart beat in her throat, and she swallowed down what felt like brightness, the light pulsing in her chest. Turning a little, she saw the Earth in the far, two-days away distance. All she could ever really do, or be, was on that speck. Forsythe might think that there was life away from the planet, and maybe in some other century there would be. He could wave his magic wand, but there would be no magic. No music. All they'd done these past days was bring all their earth shit up to the moon and deal with it. She'd been with the rich and the famous and the smart, and when it came down to all the nothing around them, they were nothing. No amount of sex—especially the kind Max barely remembered—could make them more human. More real. Nothing they'd done in the shuttle or moon unit was more than flailing. They were inconsequential. Specks. Dots. Periods. Commas. Apostrophes. Sand. Lint. Dust. Dust and more dust.

On the blue and white planet where they'd lived their whole lives, though, they were people. Connected. Whole and true and terribly broken. But whole and home.

Reaching over across the seats, she grabbed Bruce's mitted hand, large and heavy and cumbersome. But solid. True. The real lottery of infinitesimal atmosphere, that tiny skin giving them all a chance.

Max squeezed Bruce as she stared through the darkness that stretched between the shuttle and earth; through the swirl of cloud, light blue, indigo, forest greens, browns of every shade, down through the sky to the ground, into her very house, into the brightness of things. All her precious gifts—her father's baton tucked safely in her underwear drawer, her wedding ring in the clam shell on the bathroom counter, her coffee mug by her computer and manuscripts. Her people. Her husband and children, asleep in their beds. There she would be. There. That was the red arrow on the poster. There. She was there.

THE SIWC STORYTELLER'S AWARD

Michelle Barker

The annual Surrey International Writers' Conference is a high-light of the writing season for many authors, and one reason is the fiction contest judged by Jack Whyte and Diana Gabaldon. Named The Storyteller's Award, the winner must prove themselves to be adept not only in advanced wordcraft but also in spelling an audience with sheer story. Our congratulations go to the 2017 winner, Michelle Barker, for taking home this coveted $1000 prize. Michelle lives and writes in Vancouver, BC, where she also edits and teaches workshops. Her newest novel, The House of One Thousand Eyes, will be published by Annick Press in September 2018. Please visit her website at michellebarker.ca and find her on Twitter: @MBarker_190 or Facebook: Michelle Barker author.

MVP

It was Yom Kippur, the Day of Atonement, so I was supposed to be thinking about my sins. That was why I was fasting, and why I'd taken the day off at the hospital. Well, I took the day off because Goldstein was taking the day off; it wouldn't have looked good if he showed up at synagogue while I went to work.

All right, so: the low points of my year. The Blue Jays, obviously. You couldn't be a Canadian baseball fan anymore without cheering for an American team, which felt a bit disloyal. I'd opted for Seattle, since my wife singlehandedly kept their shoe stores in business. Why couldn't she buy her shoes in Vancouver like every other sane woman? It was one of those questions I didn't ask, because it led to a more terrible question: why had I married her?

The rabbi was talking about golden calves, which was ironic considering all the BMWs in the parking lot. My stomach grumbled. Fasting probably wasn't the best idea, but it was Yom Kippur. You fasted. Goldstein was fasting. I knew this because all day yesterday he'd made stupid jokes with the nurses like, "Save me a cinnamon bun, because tomorrow I starve." He was one of those guys, a kibitzer with the nurses. Not all doctors were. I thought it sent the wrong message.

The nurses liked Goldstein better than me. He was growing a beard, and it was coming in dark and full and made him look like a rabbi, which was what they called him. "Put in a good word for me at synagogue, Rabbi," they'd say, as if he had a direct line to God—except he probably did. Whatever. The truth was, I'd had a cup of coffee this morning because there were limits, and I figured God would understand given the hours I kept at the hospital.

"For the mistakes we committed before You through confusion of the heart," intoned the cantor.

Fucking Jeff Goldstein, thumping his chest after each sin like Tarzan. What did he have to be sorry for? The guy went to Africa every year to fix cleft palates.

The rabbi had already explained that in order to get any mercy from God, you first had to confess to the person you'd hurt and ask forgiveness from them.

I glanced at my wife. Honey, the truth is … The truth is, Ty Cobb was the best ball player ever, even if he was a racist, and anyway, what did racism have to do with baseball?

I looked at my watch. Goldstein's girls had brought colouring books and were actually using them. My twin boys were kicking the bench in front of us. The old man sitting there kept turning around to glare at them.

The boys were five, and Melissa had dressed them in identical suits and ties, which made them look like miniature tycoons. When the congregation fell silent, Mikey chose that as his moment to yell, "Flob!" which was one of his words that meant a variety of things, depending. Right now it probably meant,

Why did you bring me here? I'm too young for this shit. I wished I could yell it, too.

Goldstein gave me his beneficent smile, like everything is just so fine, even your two obnoxious boys who should only be allowed out in public on leashes are fine, and what's especially fine is that they're yours and not mine. See my girls? Sharing crayons.

Dr Weisberg, that was what the nurses called me — not Aaron, or Wise Guy, or Doc. It was respectful. But sometimes I wished someone would call me Rabbi, even though I wasn't growing a beard and had nothing in common with rabbis — unless they happened to be rabbis who cheated on their wives.

Finally it was time for the break. We pretended to visit with the Goldsteins, coats draped over the backs of benches, wives giving each other the painted-nail display, Goldstein asking who won the World Series this year, like, are you kidding, don't you know it hasn't started yet, the Goldstein girls eyeing the twins, one of them trying to figure out the meaning of flob, was it Hebrew, was it French, the other keeping her distance, as if she still remembered the time Mikey had thrown a miniature metal car at her head when he was two.

I hoped Goldstein was going home. If he was staying at shul all afternoon, I would have to stay too, and I wasn't in the mood for the book of Jonah. I'd never gotten the point of telling the story from inside a whale. But no, thank God, he picked up his coat, and Melissa kissed the air between them goodbye. I held my coat under one arm and Mikey under the other like a football, while he screamed "Flob!" and Melissa went red.

By the time we got home I'd decided I wasn't waiting until sundown to eat. I made myself a ham sandwich in protest. The kitchen looked like a demilitarized zone because Melissa had decided she didn't like the way the black marble countertops created glare.

"I can't cook." As if she ever cooked. She bought things at Kaplan's Deli and heated them up.

I'd left my jacket draped on a kitchen chair, and when Melissa approached I expected a theatrical sigh because she was the one who always had to hang things up. Instead, she said, "This isn't your jacket."

I put down my sandwich. She was right. I took the jacket from her and fished inside the breast pocket where most men kept a business card, the professional equivalent of writing your name on the collar in permanent marker. Yes, there was a card: Dr Jeffrey Goldstein, MD ASS.

"Jeff and I must have taken each other's coats," I said. "We'll switch them at the hospital tomorrow."

Melissa went upstairs to change. I eyed the coat. It was nicer than mine. The leather was a better quality, I could smell it.

No question of keeping it, of course, which was too bad. I held it up, shook it a little, and a clink of loose change came from one of the pockets. Without thinking, I reached inside just to see, since Goldstein had probably already checked mine, and then I wracked my memory for what I'd left in there, maybe a receipt or two from lunches with Hanna, but her name wouldn't be on them, it was nothing incriminating.

The pocket of loose change also contained a pen—expensive, I could tell because it was heavy—nail clippers (who carried nail clippers in their pocket?); a small soft cloth for cleaning glasses. In the other pocket was a granola bar that looked like it had been through the wash. A used Kleenex, well, that served me right.

There was also a little zipper pocket on the side. I unzipped it and stuck my hand in. What was this? I pulled out a plastic bag with a small amount of white powder in it. Curve ball! I put the bag back into the pocket. Took it out again. Opened it, and sniffed, but what did I know? It wasn't sugar, and I was betting it wasn't flour or baking powder either.

I should never have looked, that's what.

What I could do was pretend not to know. I hadn't looked. "Here's your jacket back, buddy, didn't even check the pockets, not that I would, I mean, what does the rabbi have to hide?"

All those deep knee bends in shul this morning. Shit. I'd always thought it would be so great to have some dirt on Goldstein, something I could whisper to the nurses, or even something I could just know, by myself, like one of those sour candies you can suck on for hours.

Now what? Goldstein would want his jacket back. Did I say anything about the bag? Of course not. The pocket had been zipped. Admitting I'd unzipped it and looked meant telling the guy I was interested in his secrets (which I was) and looking for a way to sewer him (which I thought I was, but wasn't). I wasn't one of those people who'd wanted harsh punishment when A-Rod had admitted to using steroids. It just made me sad.

What was the right thing to do? Goldstein and I weren't good enough friends to have a heart-to-heart about this, the shoulder-patting, "Hey man, you wanna talk about it?" crap they wrote about in those faygeleh men's magazines in the hospital waiting room. We were more like rivals — but not real rivals, not rivals like an anonymous call to the College of Physicians and Surgeons: "It might be affecting his work." I could never do that.

Only there was a part of me that was maybe a little satisfied. Dr Jeffrey Goldstein had something to atone for after all.

I stuffed the bag back into the pocket and zipped it shut. I put the jacket on—I couldn't help myself, I wanted to see what it felt like—and called up the stairs, "I'm going out for a bit." Got into my car and drove to Hanna's, which was a totally inappropriate place to be on Yom Kippur but whatever, God already knew I wasn't sorry for sleeping with my sister's best friend. I should have married Hanna when I'd had the chance. I was an idiot, had always been too afraid of what my sister would think. For that, I was sorry.

Hanna was a writer who had the unusual luxury of being able to stay home and not make a living at her writing, thanks to a timely inheritance. Showing up at her door unannounced was a guaranteed way to piss her off. I hesitated, then pressed the apartment buzzer and waited.

She would look out her window to see who was there before she answered. I'd seen her do it. I wondered if she'd pretend not to be home when she saw it was me.

"Why didn't you call first?" Her voice came through the intercom.

"It's important. Can I come up?"

A sigh. The buzzer.

The hallways in her building smelled of laundry detergent and some terrible stew involving cabbage and root vegetables, but Hanna wouldn't move because the rent was cheap and there was a great café around the corner that sold the best poppyseed bagels in the city.

She was wearing sweatpants and a large T-shirt, oh God, no bra, I couldn't sleep with her today. I focused on the coffee cup in her hand, the cigarette smouldering on the kitchen table next to her notebook and pen. She wrote her first drafts in longhand, which meant she was in the middle of a first draft, which meant she didn't want to see me, not now.

She narrowed her eyes. "That's not your jacket."

"I know."

I unzipped the pocket and pulled out the baggie. "Can you tell me what this is?" My nerdy teenaged years flashed past me. While everyone else had been out getting high, I'd been memorizing Yoda's dialogue from *The Empire Strikes Back*.

Hanna raised one pierced eyebrow. "Gee, Aaron. Wait. Is it cocaine?" She took the plastic bag out of my hand, licked the tip of her pinkie, and dipped it in. Touched the powder to her tongue and smiled. "Are we taking a walk on the wild side, Dr Weisberg?"

"Don't be ridiculous. It's not mine."

"That's what I used to say to my Aunt Judy."

I told her what had happened. "What do I do?"

She had that smile on her face like something was really funny to her, only I knew from experience I wouldn't find it funny at all.

"You make a big deal out of shit, you know that?" she said.

"This is a big deal. The guy's a plastic surgeon, Hanna. He operates on kids."

She shrugged. "Look, either leave it in the pocket and say nothing, or keep it and see what he does. Option A is boring but safe. It won't get you into any trouble. Option B would be more fun, but you're the one who has to work with him. Does he have a sense of humour?"

About this? I was guessing no. I stuffed the baggie back into the pocket, left the jacket on the chair, and went to use Hanna's bathroom. The tiny room was dominated by Robert Doisneau's

The Kiss by the Hôtel de Ville, which Hanna had purposely hung above the toilet to annoy her older sister, who'd given it to her as a birthday present.

By the time I came out again, I had made my decision. Option A. Door Number One, as it would have been called on the game shows my mother used to watch, *The Price Is Right* or something. Sometimes you got lucky and it was a fancy car or a great vacation behind the door; sometimes you didn't, and the door opened and there was a goat standing there tethered to the stage with its creepy eyes, looking around like what the fuck am I doing on this television show? You didn't even get to take the goat home.

I had a pretty good idea of what was behind Door Number One, in this case: the hospital where Goldstein and I worked. Medicine was a small world, and making enemies was never a good idea. I'd pretend not to know about the cocaine and hope Goldstein didn't do anything profoundly stupid or dangerous at work.

And if it was one of my boys the rabbi was operating on? All right, maybe I didn't completely know what was behind Door Number One, but it was better than the alternative.

When my hand accidentally on purpose grazed one of Hanna's loose breasts, she put down her coffee and led me to the bedroom. So much for atonement. By the time I left the apartment, the little pocket on Goldstein's coat was firmly zipped. I called him when I got home and we laughed about the mix-up in jackets. The following day we made the exchange, and everything went back to the way it had been before: Goldstein kibitzing with the nurses, me all Dr Can't Take a Joke, sometimes calling Melissa to say I'd be late and then stopping on my way home to fool around with Hanna.

Except.

Except what do you do when you know something you shouldn't? How do you *not* look at that person differently? When Goldstein came to work with a runny nose, I had to hold back the smirk. I watched the jacket's zippered pocket for signs of—I didn't know what. You can't help those things; when you know something, it's like cooking with the glare from a black marble countertop. (Maybe Melissa wasn't so crazy).

I was at Hanna's early one evening, and she was preparing dinner and listening to Rossini, that overture that always made me think of Bugs Bunny in *The Rabbit of Seville*, when she said, "What did that guy ever say about his jacket?" And she started to laugh.

"What's funny?" Did she know Goldstein? Might she and Goldstein ever have...? Unthinkable. "He didn't say anything."

"I bet he didn't. I took the baggie out before you left."

I felt like I was in one of my old Archie comics, a bubble over my head with nothing in it. She was bent over double, she was laughing so hard. She opened a drawer in her shitty little kitchen—the drawers and cupboards didn't even have handles, you had to reach under and pull them out from the bottom—and she took out the baggie and slid it across the counter.

I stared at it. "Why would you do that?"

"Relax. I thought it would be funny."

I felt like upending her pot of ratatouille on the floor. See how funny that was. I held the bag flat in my hand. "What am I supposed to do with it now?"

Hanna stirred her stew. "Slip it back into his pocket when he's not around. Or wait, here's a news flash. Take him aside and ask him about it. Tell him you've been waiting for him to bring it up and since he hasn't, you are. Be a mensch."

I gulped the last of my white wine and tucked the plastic bag in my jacket pocket. Fine. I would speak to Goldstein privately. There was no sense in humiliating the guy. If he had a drug problem, the nurses didn't need to know about it. Goldstein would be grateful. He'd owe me.

I went home, hung my jacket in the closet for once, played Lego with my boys and tried to explain to them the concept of the batting average. It was the weekend, and I wasn't on call, and the weather promised to be good enough to play catch in the park. I managed to forget all about Goldstein and the baggie until Monday morning when I went to take my jacket from the closet — and it wasn't there.

"Melissa?" I yelled. "Where's my jacket?"

"I dropped it at the cleaner's. You've been asking me to do it for days, if you remember. Thank you, honey, you're so considerate. Don't mention it."

The cleaners. My skin went prickly. What was their policy on finding illegal drugs in someone's pocket? And what was the protocol on claiming your illegal drugs? Well. I wouldn't claim them, that's what. There went the jacket. The leather was worn at the elbows anyhow, it was no great loss. I'd tell Melissa I would pick it up, a magnanimous gesture for once in my life, and then I just … wouldn't. I'd tell her they lost the damn jacket, those idiots, time we switched drycleaners anyway, we're never going back there again.

As it turned out, the cleaners' policy on finding illegal drugs in someone's pocket was to call the police. They were waiting for me in my office at the hospital, everyone silent as I walked in, nurses peering from around their station. Good morning Dr Weisberg, have we got a surprise for you.

I entered the small office and shut the door. I felt suddenly conspicuous—the scent of my expensive shower gel, the gold watch on my wrist, Zitelli and Davis's *Atlas of Pediatric Physical Diagnosis* on the shelf behind me, photographs of Melissa and the twins. Handmade cards from patients. Flob. It was a great word.

One of the policemen stood beside the desk as casually as a person can stand with a nightstick in their belt loop. The other was holding the baseball I'd had signed by Edgar Martinez.

"It isn't mine," I said to the policemen.

"What, the baseball?"

"You know," I said.

"We don't," said the policeman near the desk. "But you're going to tell us."

I sat down. *Goldstein, you schmuck.* How could he have put me in this position? I couldn't *not* tell them about him, but if I did, everyone would hate me for it. Damn. I spread my hands out on the desk. Bad idea—they were shaking.

"Listen," I said.

The door burst open, and there was Jeff Goldstein looking not guilty or repentant or any of the things I might have expected. What was written across his face was actual concern.

"There's been a terrible misunderstanding." He shut the door. The cocaine had come from a teenager, a patient. "It was one of those things, happened quickly. You have to understand how busy we are here, officers." Goldstein had meant to get rid of it or call the police or something, but then it was Yom Kippur and they'd been at shul and the jackets had gotten mixed up and he'd forgotten about it. Hadn't even noticed the jacket exchange.

"Are you saying Dr Weisberg took your jacket to the cleaners without knowing?" asked one of the officers.

Barely a second's hesitation. "That's exactly what I'm saying," said Goldstein. "They're identical. He wouldn't have known. I didn't even know until this moment."

I kept my gaze on the desk. The police said they'd have to file a report. They wanted the name of the teenager, which Goldstein refused to give them. The kid had promised to stop using. That bag had been the last of it, which was why he'd given it to Goldstein.

"Patient-doctor confidentiality, officers," he added. "You don't want to mess with that."

When the police finally left, Goldstein shut the door behind them.

I forced myself to look at him. "Thanks. I mean——"

"Why didn't you come to me when you'd found it in my pocket? I really had forgotten about it, you know. It wasn't until I heard the police were here—and I knew you couldn't have done anything wrong—that I remembered the bag. Why didn't you say something?"

I shook my head. "I couldn't. I didn't know what to think. I assumed——"

Third year in a row the National League had won the All-Star Game, you couldn't even call it a game, 8-0, it was a skunk, that's what, a total faceplant.

THE 2017 RAVEN
SHORT STORY CONTEST

THE 2017 RAVEN SHORT STORY CONTEST

With so many unique and gifted writers, 2017's Raven Contest was difficult to judge, and we would like to thank Brenda Carre for her appraising eye. Her words on the selected winners' short stories will whet your appetite ...

First Place: Elaine McDivitt, 'The Tape'

"Who does not remember the striking cover of The Female Eunuch *by Germaine Greer? It provided a visual punch that the story made good on right to the end. I found the circular theme of tape in Virginia's haunting narration a gripping read. The unique cadence really supported the sense of horror and realization unlocked at a garage sale."*

— *Brenda Carre*

Second Place: Kerry Craven, 'Meggie'

"This was a very interesting fairy-tale-esque exploration of the dehumanization of dementia. Through Meggie's surprising transformation into a new being she is able to move past grief at least for awhile. I loved the Baba Yaga quality of the magical young woman with the sack full of all possibilities."

— *Brenda Carre*

Runner Up: Alex Reece Abbott, 'My Brother Paulie: A Domestic Space Odyssey'

"My Brother Paulie was a very short, tight flash piece exploring the narrator's somewhat whimsical and rather dark understanding of her brother's 'altered state' of consciousness. I liked the 'Major Tom' overtones."

— *Brenda Carre*

Runner Up: Charity Tahmaseb, 'The Potato Bug War'

"I loved the symbolic nature of the sacrificed potato bugs in this piece. I enjoyed the young teacher's defiance against all odds. A few details needed more clarification for me, but otherwise a nice piece of flash fiction."

Brenda Carre

November 2017

Congratulations to all of these writers! Pulp Literature Press is grateful for the abundance of talent and hard work that was poured into all of the submissions for the 2017 Raven Short Story Contest. Published here, in Issue 18, are first and second place winners for the 2017 Raven Short Story Contest, 'The Tape' by Elaine McDivitt and 'Meggie' by Kerry Craven.

Elaine McDivitt *is a full-time partner in a landscaping business that grows perennials for garden centres. Her past includes fifteen years of training race-horses. She has two adult children who recall their mother constantly reading to them and to herself. Nine years ago she pursued her passion for writing by taking the Humber College mentor program. She loves her book club so much she works her holidays around it.*

THE TAPE

It was a dull, humid Saturday in September. Virginia was in town visiting her mother, who still lived in the same suburban house that Virginia had grown up in. The sun was breaking as Virginia laced up her runners and left for a long overdue homecoming tour of the neighbourhood. The houses seemed smaller every time she came home, the trees either larger or gone altogether. The environmentalist inside Virginia winced and wondered why the town was not replanting. The sidewalks, where there were some, meandered around and over the topography of aged tree roots and nudged the edges of newer pavestone driveways. An upscale neighbourhood when it was built in the 50s, the area was now spilling with wealthy homeowners keen to renovate and commute. Of all of Virginia's childhood friends, not one had remained or returned to live in these old stomping grounds. The lure of the city had been strong. Her mother was the last of the parents hanging on, refusing to leave and content to complain about the constant comings and goings of trades people up and down the street. Virginia walked for an hour, musing about the changes inside these homes.

On the way back, she turned down the street one over from her mother's and saw, midway down, pink neon cardboard signs screaming 'Yard Sale'. Virginia knew the house. Early birds were prowling the finds. As she got closer she could see the usual racks of clothes lining the driveway. A few lamps, an overstuffed chair, random golf clubs. A blender with a note saying, 'Works!' The lawn was littered with children's items: a baby swing, a high chair, boxes of plastic toys. The Ozgas had lived here when Virginia was a child, but they had long ago moved away. She looked at the house and the stone façade was familiar, timeless. It had been, what? Forty-five years or more since she'd been inside.

These people were at least the second family since the Ozgas. Her attention was caught by the requisite yard sale stack of paperbacks with cracked spines and ruffled edges. They sat piled on a small IKEA dresser. Virginia like to flip through books at yard sales, finding them to be a window to the souls of the sellers. Moving closer, she could see they were mostly recent and what she classified as 'beach reads'. Mysteries, thrillers, a little romance. Some bestsellers were among them. Just a slice of one book cover in the stack drew her attention. The slice was enough to define the book as out of place. Virginia glanced around, looking for a possible former owner. She slid the book out with a kind of reverence, and saw the familiar title: *The Female Eunuch* by Germaine Greer.

A guy with a trim, close beard and fitted T-shirt appeared across the table from Virginia, his hands in mock self-defence, smiling. "Ah. That book. Fifty cents?" He stepped from foot to foot, watching Virginia's face.

"Hmm, oh, I was just ... just drawn by the jacket," Virginia said, a little distractedly. "I've actually read it. Long ago. School." She ran a finger along the front cover and the iconic image of a naked female torso hanging from a horizontal clothing pole. Its savagery and vulnerability gave Virginia pause the same way it had years before. She was aware of her revulsion at the stark violence of the artwork and yet also experienced an empowering sense of being part of a new paradigm, a new age, a rising-up.

"Oh yeah?" He wanted the sale. "I know nothing about it." He shifted from foot to foot. "It was in a box of stuff in the basement when we bought the house, and, well, it finally made it out here." He waved vaguely at the yard sale, his awkwardness squatting between them. Virginia almost smiled, pondering what he thought, or had once thought, the jacket promised. She was pretty sure he had been disappointed. She wanted to ask how long ago he had bought the house but did not. Curiosity pulled, and she flipped the cover open. Inside the front page was some small, tight writing. She squinted to read it. The guy was called to the Lego table and Virginia stuck her face closer to decipher the wording. Her lips moved slowly, a habit she'd never tried to break, and a quiver lit up her spine.

"I have to aGreer with you on this one ... David Ozga." A smiley face was drawn beside his name.

Pins and needles crept up her hands and wrists, and she put the book down as she sought some congruity with the name, the book, her memory. She flexed her hands, wriggled her fingers, and walked away from the yard sale, distractedly noticing the boulevard didn't have white chrysanthemums and showy purple asters planted this fall. Too late now, winter was on the way. This warm fall could turn to snow at any moment. Montreal was like that. Virginia triggered a memory, a trickle, a surging-to-the-surface type memory, the kind that you try to drown but that floats back to the surface because the concrete block it's tied to has rotted away.

The Ozga kids went to the public school, an anomaly among families on their Irish-Catholic street, enough that they were not part of the general childhood gang. In the very hot summer of 1971, Virginia's best friend, Paula, was away on a family vacation. Virginia spent hours idly riding her Mustang bike up and down the street and around the block. Going by the Ozgas' one day, Sandi, who was one year older than nine-year-old Virginia, was hula-hooping in the driveway.

"Hey!" Sandi called out to Virginia, who was lazily back-pedalling, pretending not to be staring.

Virginia watched as the hula hoop beat around Sandi's knees at a wicked pace before clattering to the pavement. Sandi gave a dramatic sigh. Nervous, Virginia turned her bike and stopped. It was not common to hang around kids outside your grade or school.

"I'll show you," Sandi said. And she did.

Late that afternoon, Sandi's older sister, Dana, came home from her summer job at the pool, then David arrived on his ten-speed bike and disappeared into the back yard.

For three days Virginia showed up at Sandi's house. Both of Sandi's parents worked. Dana worked afternoons at the pool, David at a bike shop all day. Sandi was left alone for three hours in the afternoon. Virginia would not tell her mother this. Sandi's house was another world.

They played with Dana's makeup, whispering even though no one else was in the house. Sandi was sure to 'get rid of all the evidence', because she said Dana would 'have a freak out' if she knew. They tried on Dana's clothes, halter tops with fringes and beads and bra cups that they stuffed with washcloths or Kleenex. In the basement, they danced to David's records, Sandi showing Virginia how to move 'sexy'. Over and over Sandi would play 'Wild Thing' by The Troggs. She had a T-shirt on which her mother had glued sequins that spelled out wild.

On day three, Dana left for work early, her boyfriend picking her up. Sandi and Virginia played Barbie goes on dates, which involved lots of clothes changing, sassy talk, and kissing the Ken doll. Virginia came early and stayed for lunch. They ate an entire roll of chocolate chip cookie dough. Then, Sandi had a plan:

"Let's pretend to be mummies."

Sandi pulled Virginia by the hand to the basement. She dug into David's hockey bag and held up rolls of black hockey tape. It was the wide, sticky kind for the blade of the stick. Sandi rambled about how cool it would feel to be wrapped like a mummy. Virginia felt sweaty.

Methodically, with a ten-year-old's precision, Sandi wrapped Virginia in the tape, starting with her head. The tape wouldn't stick tight, so she paused. "Wait," she said. "Don't move." Then Sandi rummaged in a box at the bottom of the stairs and pulled out a bathing cap, orange, with the chin strap broken off. She helped Virginia tug it on and stuff her ponytail up the back. Back to wrapping, Sandi left room around the eyes, the nose, and the mouth and started on the neck. Virginia willed herself to be still. Halfway from chin to collarbone Virginia got panicky. She sucked air in hard through her mouth and asked Sandi to stop.

"It's okay," said Sandi, continuing to pull the tape and wind it around Virginia's neck. "This is the hardest part, and it's done."

Starting another roll of tape, Sandi said she would do the arms. Virginia wanted to cross her hands over her chest, but the tape wouldn't stick right because of her shirt. Sandi said the only way to do it right was for Virginia to take off her shirt and have her hands by her sides. She said she would leave her fingers out. So Virginia did those things. The tape felt cold on her chest and tummy as Sandi made her way from shoulders to shorts. Again, the tape wouldn't stick.

"You have to take your shorts off," Sandi said. Virginia couldn't do it with her arms taped to her sides.

"Here, I'll help you," said Sandi. Virginia let her. Sandi slid Virginia's underpants off too. Virginia felt hot and dizzy as Sandi wound the tape around her hips, across her bum and a little bit down her thighs. Then there was not enough tape.

"I'm almost done," Sandi said. She did two more rounds, a little bit looser, and it was the end of the tape. She stood back to admire her work.

"You look just like a mummy," she said, producing a mirror that Virginia hadn't previously noticed.

"What about you?" Virginia squeaked, realizing at that moment that not only was there no more tape but her hands were strapped to her sides. Fear stopped her from saying she was afraid.

"I'll have to do it next time," said Sandi. "Or maybe we can use the same tape when we take it off."

In the silence that followed, Virginia worked to keep herself from crying, and Sandi twirled Virginia around slowly for a better look. They both heard the door to the basement open, and Sandi's eyes went wide. David's voice floated down,

"Hey Sandi, you down there?" He was home early.

Virginia had not seen Sandi look worried before now. Sandi put a finger to her mouth, "Shhh."

"Sandi?" His voice was a little louder. The door shut again, and they listened to his footsteps as he travelled through the living room. They heard him run up the second-floor stairs, calling out.

"You have to hide," Sandi said with urgency. She looked around, pointed to the toy box, and quickly pulled the stuffed animals out. Virginia didn't want to get in the toy box. She could hardly move her upper body. Sandi whispered with a panicky tone to get in. Virginia's fingers were free, so she could grip the sides of the toy box and lower herself inside. The tape cut into her when she bent her knees. Sandi pulled the lid down, and Virginia began to cry in the darkness. David's voice called from the stairs again, and Sandi answered this time.

"I'm here."

David's footsteps stopped partway down the stairs. Virginia could hear Sandi breathing and could hear her feet shuffling the toy animals.

"Why didn't you answer me?" he asked. Without waiting for a reply he said, "I've got early practice today. I'll get you something to eat before I go."

Virginia heard David's retreat up the stairs. The toy box lid opened and Sandi asked, "Do you want to come out?"

Virginia nodded, tears catching on the tape and pooling under her eyes. She couldn't pull herself up; her tightly wrapped arms made it impossible. Another wave of panic rolled through her, and she whined, "Help me."Sandi pulled on Virginia's torso. Virginia sobbed, unmoveable.

"It's okay," Sandi said. It was the voice she used when she

made Ken apologize to Barbie for something bad he had done, yet Barbie always ended up saying she was sorry instead of the other way around.

They didn't hear David on the stairs. They jolted when his voice floated over Sandi's head. "What the fuck is going on?"

He didn't yell. Virginia couldn't speak for terror. Sandi went quiet. David reached down, picked Virginia up, and set her standing on the floor. He peered into her eyes as she trembled.

"Are you all right?" he asked gently.

"We were just playing mummies," said Sandi.

David elbowed his sister and told her to go get a bowl of warm water and a facecloth. He looked again at Virginia.

"I'm going to start taking the tape off," he said. "Tell me if it hurts too much."

It hurt. The warm water helped. David was careful, and he talked to Virginia the whole time, ignoring Sandi other than to tell her to get more water. David started with her head, freeing her stoic face. The skin at her temples pricked like needles, a few loose hair strands stuck to the tape. The bathing cap came off with a sucking sound. He chided Virginia gently for letting his wild little sister talk her into something so crazy. He told Virginia a few knock-knock jokes, but she didn't get them, her mind blank. With scissors, he carefully freed her neck, cutting up the back, apologizing. He began to soak her chest and tried to pull the tape. It hurt the most. When he tugged and a nipple showed itself, dotted with blood, he stopped.

"Where's your shirt?" he asked, his voice catching. He looked around, eyes wide, and saw the blue shirt and matching blue shorts among the stuffed animals from the toy box.

The memory made Virginia shiver. She remembered David on

the phone, urgently saying, "Come home now." She remembered Dana rushing in, still in her bathing suit, a bikini with little peace signs all over it. She felt in her memory Dana's kind fingers working softly. When it was over, Dana fitted two streamers on the handlebars of Virginia's bike, a leather fringe with bright beads. They were beautiful.

"I made these," Dana said, "for Sandi. But I think she wants you to have them."

Virginia's body stung like a sunburn. The worst ever. She pushed her bike home. Did she just forget to ride it? The screen door bounced shut behind her when she slipped into the kitchen. Busy at the stove with a potato pot about to boil over, her mother lifted the lid, dialled the burner off, and said, "I think you're overdoing your welcome down there at the Ozgas' every day. Time to give it a break, don't you think? I don't know the woman, but surely she'd like a little bit of peace now and then." She replaced the pot lid, adding, "The teenage daughter — Diana, is it? No, it's something else. She looks like nothing but trouble to me. They have their hands full with her, I'm sure. Finish setting the table then call your brother. He's downstairs glued to the TV." Turning to Virginia, she paused. "What have you done to your face?" Virginia reached a hand to her burning hot face and felt a tiny piece of black tape that was still stuck to her temple.

Virginia said it was her own idea, the mummy thing. Said it was fun. She never played with Sandi again. They never really crossed paths. David was gone that fall, a hockey scholarship in Michigan, a long ten hours by car. When Virginia was shopping for fall school clothes with her mother, they saw Dana in the mall. Dana blew Virginia a kiss and winked. Virginia's mother said, "There's something different about that one."

Once again walking away from the Ozgas' childhood house, Virginia headed for home the same way she had done that day years ago. It crossed her mind that the sidewalk had not changed. She thought of Sandi, of Dana, and of the teenage boy with the gentle eyes who, at some later time, read the book with the deliberate, provocative cover. She thought he was likely a very good man.

She paused mid-block and decided to turn around and buy the book.

Kerry Craven *is an English and creative writing teacher in Oshawa, Ontario. The story 'Meggie' was written on a retreat in Scotland with Inkslingers, a local writing group. It was inspired by the brave people in her life who struggle to care for those with dementia, mental health issues, and addiction problems. As a child, her grandmother Alma Craven had a magic bag that always seemed to have something wonderful in it for her, and she looks back fondly on the days when magic still existed in her world.*

MEGGIE

She arrives in darkness. I am tending the fire, stirring the stew, when I hear the knock, like a brushing broom, against the wooden door. The stew is old, ten days at least. I can't leave mother long, so I must make do with what I have as I tend to the golem that sleeps in the corner.

I slip the rope latch and see a woman who is both the youngest and oldest person I've ever seen. She has golden-red curls and healthy round cheeks with a hint of apple blossom sweetness. "I hear yer mother is possessed," she says. "I've come to help ye." A burlap bag is slung from her shoulders. She rattles it towards me as some sort of proof of her intention. It could be a bag full of half-dead kittens for all I know, but it is dark, and the night is chill, and no stranger is ever turned away in our town.

"Come in," I say. "Come warm your feet by the fire." She settles in the low chair, pulling back her voluminous skirt to

keep it from the flames. "Here," I say. "You must be hungry."
I hand her stew in my own battered, leaky tin cup. It looks so
meagre; I am ashamed.

"Pah," she says. "This mess would hardly nourish a bag full
of kittens." I start. She gives me a wink. "Well, thas' alright,"
she says, laying her hand on my shoulder. "We all do the best
we can, don't we, dearie? So then, about yer mother."

"She's not terribly well," I say. "We should try not to wake her."

"Bah," she says. "Not terribly well? Last I heard, she was
hanging off the church steeple week afore wearing nought but
her knickers." I redden. It's true. She'd called the minister a
demonic strumpet and dumped soot on the heads of the prim
little parishioners.

The cackling laugh makes me cringe as I see my mother's
hulking mass stir in the corner.

"Good morning, Mother." A burbling emerges from the bed-
clothes. "Would you like some of the soup?" I ask.

"You're a slut," she replies.

"I put leeks in it today. Remember, you like leeks."

"Liar. I've never said any such thing, you harlot."

"Here, Mother." I prop her on her cushion. Her body is so
gentle, soft and pliable. The blue eyes plead with me. She looks
like a woman in a cage.

"My legs hurt, Meggie," she simpers. "Why do my legs hurt
so much? I can't move. There's something on my legs."

When I bring her stew, she begins to slurp it like a small
child, two hands holding the cup.

"Careful, Mother, it's hot," I say.

"Bitch!" she replies.

I return to sit with the mysterious young woman. She clucks

her tongue. Reaching into her satchel, she pulls out a cob pipe, waves it in my direction to see if I mind. I shrug. Perhaps the tobacco smell will mask the stench of the woman who slurps like an infant in the corner, pouring stew down her nightie.

The young woman puffs silently for a while, watching the sparks dance. "Here, girl," she finally asks. "Have you ever seen a magic bag?"

The satchel is plain and dun. I cock an eyebrow.

"Ah, not believing me, I see. Well, think of a treat, then. Think of the best thing you ever et, then reach in that bag and see what you find."

I have only ever had one sweet in my life, a caramel at the seaside, with my mother. Reaching into the bag, I scrounge to the bottom. The bag is empty ... and then it isn't. My fingers come upon the caramel, wrapped in wax paper. Popping it into my mouth, I try to avoid swallowing it, enjoying the tiny moment of joy.

My eyes widen further as the young woman reaches into the sack, pulls out a giant turkey leg, steaming. She sets the pipe down, rips pieces of flesh with her sharp incisors.

"But, that was empty," I say.

"Nothing is truly empty in this world," she says. As she speaks, I begin to hear bagpipes and the sounds of the seaside coming from the neck of the bag.

She gives it a rattle. "Now behave," she tells it. The piping stops with a cack. Patting the bag, she gazes into me.

"What would you say, girl," she asks, "if I told you I could give you the one thing that would make you happy? What would you say to that?"

I force a tiny smile, return my gaze to the fire. "That," I sigh, "is an impossible thing."

"Ay, ay," she says. "Quite a tricky thing, that. I'd be thinking it's freedom you're wanting. I see you as a happy, carefree creature, walking out that door, never coming back."

I give a nod and regret it almost instantly. "I could never be happy if I had to leave Mother," I say.

"That old thing?" The woman chuckles again, wedges the pipe sharply between her teeth. "That creature t'aint a bit your mother. Yer mother's sleeping like a baby somewhere inside o' there, aye, but that thing's nothing but a bloated old haggis."

"Please," I ask. "Can't you help her? Isn't there any way you can make her be her again?"

"Gor, nope. Yer mother is right where she needs to be right now. She's done, used up. There's naught for her here, b'god. She's safe and warm right where she is. You, though, young lady." She taps the chair with her pipe. "You're the one I came to help. Quite the puzzle, t'be sure." I wait for her to continue, but she merely pinches her eyes into little slits, examining me. I cough, and turn to the fire.

"Well," I say. "You'll be needing a place to sleep. The barn's clean, cleaner than here, and mother wakes through the night."

The woman springs from her chair. "The barn'll do nicely, thank you kindly." She walks to the door, turns to take one last look through the cottage. "Yarp. Quite the puzzle, indeed." Grinning broadly, she slips open the neck of the bag, just a bit, and whispers into it. I think I hear the bag whisper back. A gust of wind blows in as she opens the door and leaves. I feel the whispers rushing against my face, through my hair. Tiny whispers, like tiny kisses. The door slams shut behind her.

Nothing left now but Mother and me.

Mother doesn't wake, not once. I used to sleep next to her in the bed, but lately I've been sleeping curled up by the fire. The grey embers settle down and cool, but it is not long before I begin to feel the sun through the window and wake to hear the door crash open. The young woman bangs through, her face full of mischief. I crack one eye, but I am too sleepy, too warm. I could sleep all day, but then suddenly I remember again. Mother. She didn't wake. Not once. The young woman smiles as I dart up on all fours, my back arched. "Aye, Meggie girl. Quite a problem you posed to me. So what do you think of the solution?"

"Mew," I say. Wrinkling my nose, I try again. "Mew." I stretch one tiny velvet paw in front of me, mottled orange and black. There is a speck of ash. I lick it off, then stick out my tongue at the taste. Spinning around, I catch sight of an orange tail, striped and fluffy and bright.

The woman laughs again, picks me up by the scruff of my neck, and brings me close to her nose. I'm barely as big as her hand. I have a whole new life ahead of me. "So now, dear creature, I'll give you a choice. The first real choice you've ever had. But first, it's time to deal with yer poor dear mother." She places me on top of mother's legs. I walk gently up to her chest. Her breaths are shallow. "There, girl, you know what to do. It's what you poor dear critters are made for." I pad up to mother's mouth, so gently. Her eyes flutter open. I can smell the number of breaths she has, and I know there are not many left. Her eyes though, so blue, so clouded, they know me. I lean my tiny forehead against her face. With the last of her strength, she gently pushes back with her own soft face. Reaching my mouth to hers, I suck out her final words, sweet words that only a mother could know. I will take her with me when I go.

I turn to the young woman, swish my tail, push my back against her warm hand. "Ay now, girl, well done. That's the way. Now, here's your choice." She holds up the bag, a bag full of everything. A bag full of imagination. "D'you come with me, d'you see the world, safe and protected?" I give an indignant sneeze. "Aye, I thought not. Or you can forge out in the world alone, face the risks. Take your chances. You might find happiness, or you might not, but you'll do it alone, with naught to tie you down."

I pounce to the ground, preen against the splintered wood door. "Meeeooow," I tell her, my eyes alert. Somewhere in the field, I smell a mouse. The hunt is on.

"Aye," the young woman replies. "I thought that's what you'd say." She pulls the latch, and sunlight streams into the room. As she throws her satchel over her shoulder, I hear tiny mews. "Ach," she tells the bag. "Behave in there, all of you." We stride through the cabin door together, but I quickly dash ahead, into a great and open world.

BONE DRY

Roy Gray and
Ben Baldwin

Roy Gray's short writings and poetry have appeared in magazines, anthologies, and online journals. Another Roy Gray writes erotic poetry online — do not confuse them. Roy's chapbook *The Joy of Technology* (Pendragon Press, 2011 — now a self-published ebook) could persuade some he is that other, but this Roy's poetic efforts remain decidedly chaste. 'Bone Dry' is his first successful graphic short story.

Ben Baldwin is a self-taught freelance artist from the UK who works with a combination of traditional media, photography, and digital art programs. He has been shortlisted for the British Fantasy Award for Best Artist for the last seven years and has also been shortlisted for the British Science Fiction Association Award for Best Artist. You can find out more about Ben and his work at benbaldwin.co.uk.

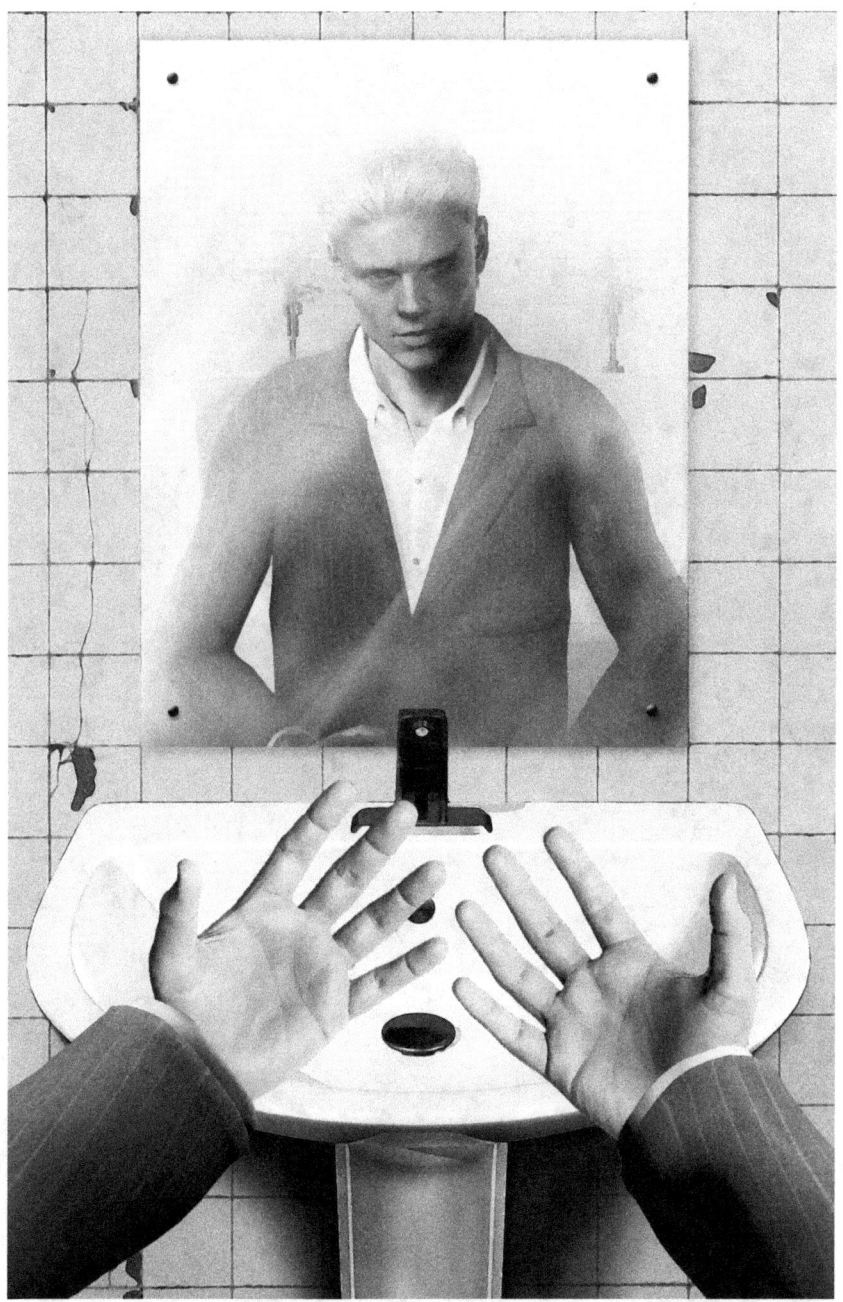

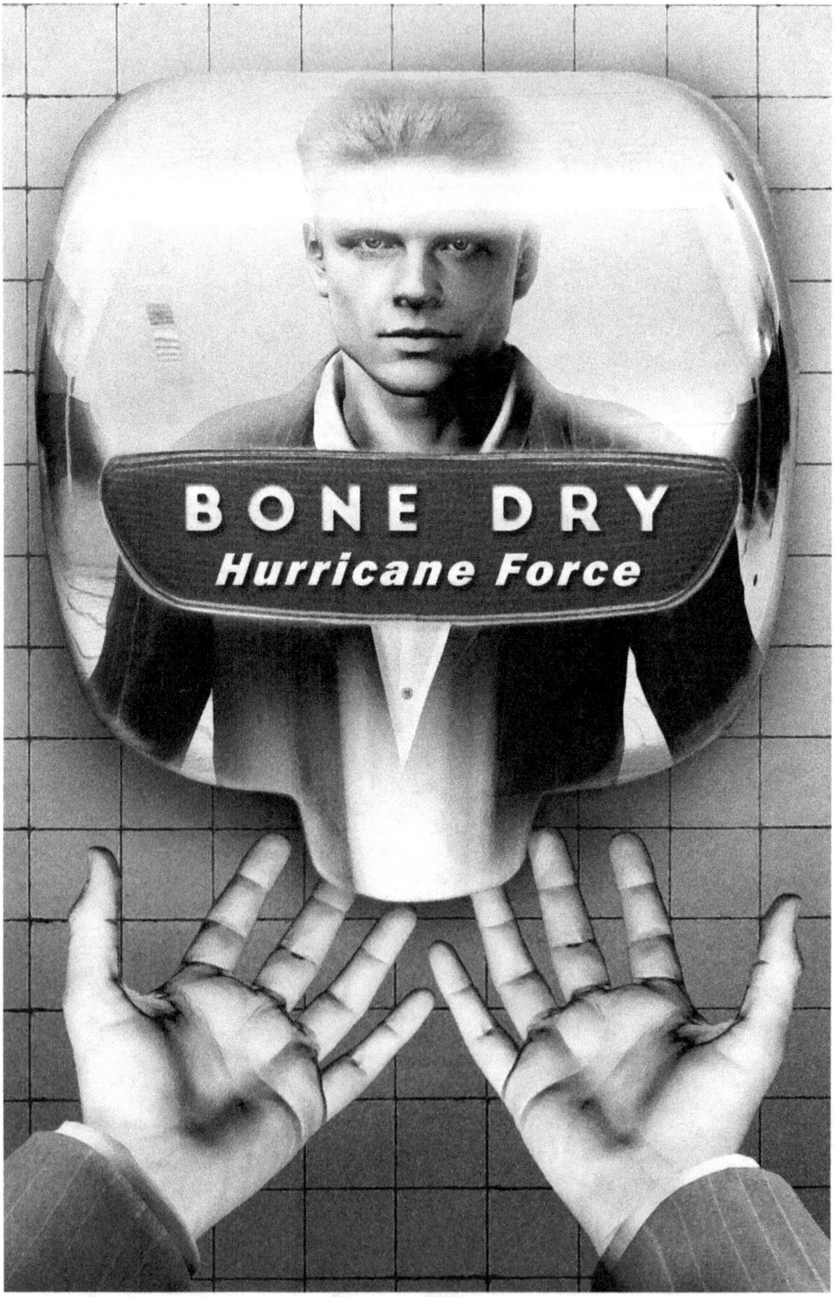
BONE DRY
Hurricane Force

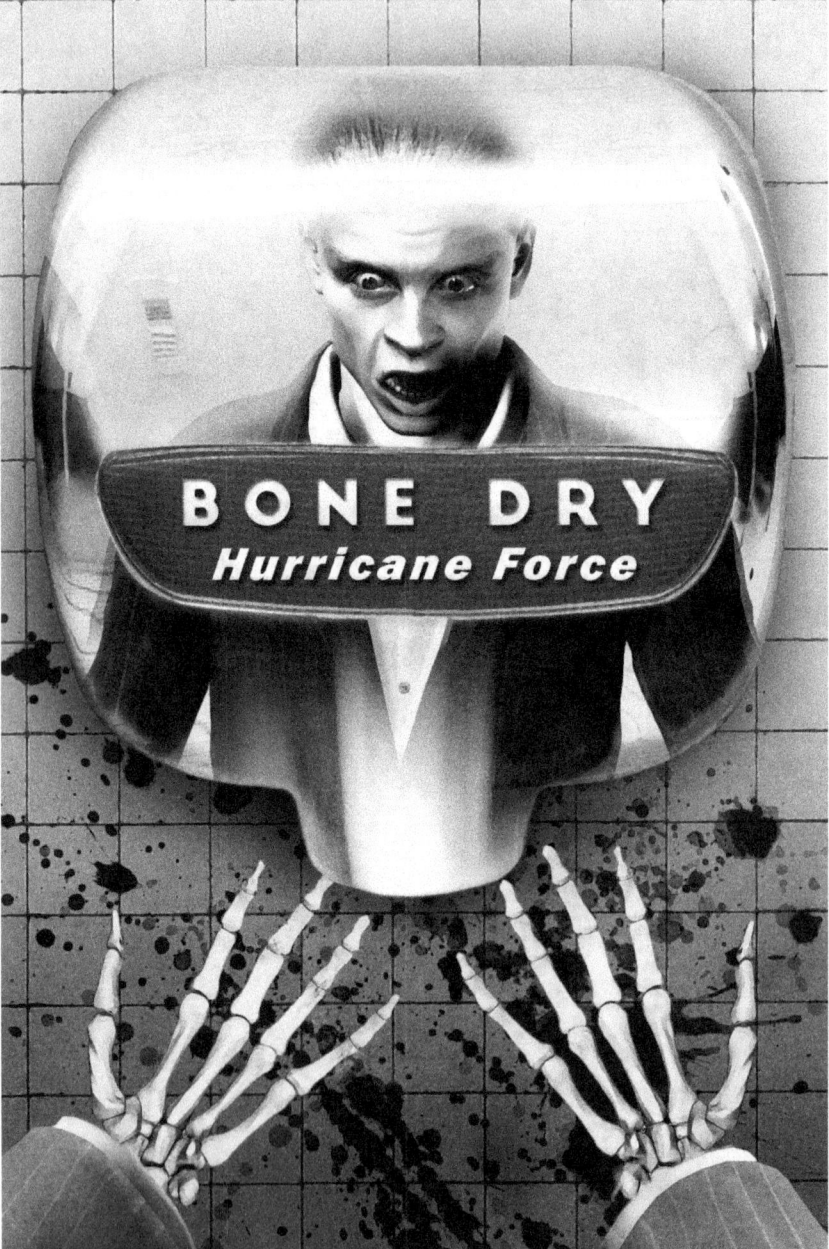

ALLAIGNA'S SONG: ARIA

JM Landels

Allaigna's Song: Aria *is the second novel in the Allaigna's Song trilogy by equestrian swordswoman, artist, and editor* **JM Landels**. *The first book,* Overture, *was printed serially in issues 1 through 11 of* Pulp Literature, *and is now available in a single volume from Pulp Literature Press and Amazon.*

$\mathscr{P}$REVIOUSLY IN ALLAIGNA'S SONG ...

Fleeing an unwanted betrothal and enraged by her family's lies concerning her parenthood, fourteen-year-old Allaigna has set off to find her true father. However, her quest is interrupted a mere three days in when a chance encounter lands her in the illegal poaching encampment of her betrothed-to-be, Tiern Doniver. She is recognized but escapes, only to be brought in by Morran Rhoan, a travelling singer in the employ of Doniver.

Eleven years ago: Lauresa and her mother Irdaign have been reunited with the birth of Allaigna, and Irdaign has made herself a part of the household under the assumed name of Angeley. As Lauresa grows into her role as mother and mistress of the castle, Allaigna's life is disrupted by the birth of her brother. In the meantime Irdaign, unable by law to see her former husband, Chanist, Prince of Brandishear, attempts to wean him from drink through the proxy of Lauresa.

IRDAIGN'S CHORUS

Though I miss my daughter and grandchildren, I am glad to be in Aleran. There is a freedom to wandering the market stalls of the capital unknown and unfettered, for the time being, of responsibilities. It is not so grand or varied as Rheran, but near enough. It makes me feel almost young. For all that I have lived I'm not so old, I remind myself. Only forty-two, and thanks to Leisanmira lore and a varied and active life, not nearly so aged in appearance as many women of my years. I laugh to myself at this spark of vanity. And what good does my lingering beauty do? I have no husband or even admirer for whom to display it. I am no longer a princess, whose loveliness is needed to reflect the state of the realm. No, it is for me and me alone that I take pride in still being able to turn the heads as I walk down the street. How many grandmothers can do that?

It is a shame Chanist is not so well preserved.

The thought sobers me as I reach the inn where I've taken a room. I lay my bundles of herbs, packets of spices, buttons and coloured threads, steel needles and bottles of oils and essences on the small table. From my pack I draw the scoured brass bowl I travel with and fill it with water from the ewer on the nightstand.

It takes a while for Chanist's image to form on the surface of the water, possibly because it so little matches the face from my memory. True, he is six years my senior, but he has aged far more than that. The sandy brown of his hair has been replaced almost entirely by white, and his beard, sparse when I married him, is clipped short but covers his chin and jaw in a dense thicket.

His eyes, his lovely soft blue eyes, are the same, though they are watery and red-lined and set in flesh that pouches below and creases above. I want to see hen's feet of laughter, but instead I see lines of worry. The jaw is still strong and square, squarer perhaps, with a stubborn cast that wasn't always there. Or was it? Is my memory touched with a golden glow?

Yet despite the disservice time and care have done to this face, it still stirs me. Not with the passion of youth that made me cast my nets upon it, but with a tender desire to care for it, to nurture and heal it.

And I could. I could easily restore his looks. We Leisanmira cannot turn the hourglass upside down, as some think we can, and restore lost youth. But I could heal what damage sorrow and drink have done, and bring him to the health a forty-eight-year-old should have. But only in person. And that I cannot do. By the terms of our divorce we are allowed no contact but by written word. Breaching the terms of the divorce would allow the Lords to remove him from the throne, replace him with one of his daughters or son, or with Gwannyn, even.

Tears fall, shattering the image in the scrying bowl. For his sake I would do it. Not just for his health, but for his heart. The taste of happiness he and, I admit, I would earn if he were no longer Prince is sweet but deadly, and I will not indulge. The Ilmar needs him still.

The next time *I see him in the bowl he is in a full rage. A carafe of wine hurtles across the room, trailing pink droplets as it lands squarely in the hearth. His aim, at least, remains good.*

His squire, still cowering, skulks over to mop up the mess. Sound fades in slowly, as if approaching from afar.

". . . mind that! I said leave it, boy!" The squire jumps to his feet. "Are you a drudge or chambermaid? I said I want some decent wine, or damn it I'll have that butler striped."

The squire scurries from the room, and I am tempted to follow him with my Sight, to see what gossip ensues amongst the servants. But it takes a more skilled farseer than I to split one's attention easily, and I do not want to lose track of my former husband.

He paces the room in a stumbling, uncoordinated way, then throws himself down on the armchair. One might think him drunk, but I'm sure these are instead the signs of withdrawal.

A knock comes on the chamber door, and it opens without pause for a reply. My daughter steps in, regal, poised like the water-bearer of legend, a new pitcher in her hand.

"Lauresa, darling." Chanist rises with difficulty and comes toward her, stumbling as he negotiates the bedpost. "I don't know what's the greater treat for these tired old eyes — your lovely face or that pitcher you're holding."

She turns a cheek for him to kiss, still elegant and composed. "Well, father, I hope you treat daughters better than pitchers." She nods towards the mess in the hearth. They stare at it, both aware that he in fact treats daughters much the same.

He puts a gnarled hand on her shoulder.

"I think you should have a word with that butler of yours, dear. The swill he sends me is dreadful. I think he's watering it.

Without responding, she crosses to the sideboard and pours him a small amount from the vessel she carries. It is dark, ruby red and unwatered. And, I hope, contains my tincture.

"Ah, that is so much better . . ." He takes an appreciative swallow, draining the small cup in one gulp.

The tincture is flavourless, and he doesn't notice its presence in the wine. But when Lauresa refills the cup, he merely sips. And for the third, refuses altogether.

I hope the fortnight he is there will be enough time for the spell I sang into the tincture to work. Though it doesn't affect the taste of a drink, it affects the desire for it. If Lauresa offers him wine, mead, port, and brandy during these days, he should leave Teillai with the taste for none of them. It won't last forever, but it will help; and for now it is the best I can do.

When Chanist is gone on his way to Aleran, it is once more safe for me to return to Osthegn. I feel uneasy, a stranger in this castle I've made my home for the past four years. I tread lightly, like a cat ready to flee, and for the first time in years I feel the pull of the road, the urge to return to my travelling lifestyle. It is because things have changed here.

Lauresa is different. Sadder, more thoughtful, but also more content, and more in charge. She has at last grown into her role as mistress of this demesne. But it is not just Lauresa. It is him: his ghost, his scent, still warm in the air of the guest chamber he has vacated only two days ago. The aroma has changed but holds elements so close to the remembered scent of him it breaks my heart all over again.

I smell hers as she enters the room, that dear scent, closer even to my heart than his. But it is the sound I hear, the raindrop-like tattle of bare feet on warm stone, that roots me here.

"Jelly!" cries Allaigna as she tumbles into my arms.

"Oh, how I've missed you, my darling," I scoop her up, her tiny body settling itself comfortably astride my hip. "You will have to tell me all about your grandpapa's visit."

And so life ripples on, Chanist's wake smoothing silently back into Osthegn's daily life. Lauresa, it appears, has conceived again, a mere nine months after Allenry's birth. I chide her for not nursing Allenry enough. It seems she has hired a wet nurse to see Allenry through the night. It hasn't harmed him, for he is a robust and chubby baby, but the unintended consequence of another pregnancy is draining Lauresa.

Andreg is delighted, of course, so much so that he hasn't visited his mistress since Allenry's birth. I am not all-seeing, but of this I can be fairly sure.

But Lauresa ... Lauresa is so drawn, exhausted beyond exhaustion by a new pregnancy and a new baby all at once. She doesn't need my chiding. She realizes the effect her small holiday from maternal care has had. I can almost see the blood drain from her face as she guiltily nurses Allenry. She is so thin her belly begins to show at barely two months, a strangled lump between her belt and her bony hips. How can Andreg not see it? Why must he insist on banquet after banquet, parading his beautiful yet rake-thin wife and chubby son before his vassals? I could almost wish the borders were less quiet, to draw his noisy, overbearing presence from the household and let my daughter rest.

And Allaigna, poor Allaigna, suffers the most. Her mama has gone from her, no matter Lauresa's wishes. She hasn't the means to afford Allaigna more. At least I am here to fill in the gaps, pick up the morsels Lauresa lets fall from her plate of care. It is second-best to a mother's love, but it can be no other way. That hard little shell Allaigna is growing around her tender heart will serve her later on. She will never find it easy to love or to trust, but she will also find it hard to be hurt ... and that may be the bitter gift she needs.

VERSE 10

A DANGEROUS DINNER

I knocked on the small door at the top of the narrow passage, my fingers plucking at the waist and bodice of the ill-fitting dress. The blue and grey velvet was fine enough and the garment well made, but made for a figure other than mine. Though Doniver had judged my height well enough, the whole dress hung shapeless on my peg-like frame.

"Enter," he called at last, and I pushed open a door so small even I had to duck to enter.

The scent of roast meat and decanted wine reached my nostrils before my eyes found Tiern Doniver in the softly lit room. The sideboard was already laden with food and drink; there would be no visits from servants tonight. The thought should have relieved me on account of my new appearance as a girl, but instead it made me nervous.

Doniver had just been washing his face. His reddish hair was damp and pushed back from a shiny forehead. He wore no doublet, only breeks and an unlaced lawn shirt. He was at least wearing boots, but those too were unlaced and sagged about his ankles.

As inexperienced as I was in such matters, I was in no doubt the setting was designed for seduction of one kind or another. And if that failed … would he truly force himself on me when all he had to do was wait? I was certain my charms were insufficient to cause a man to lose his judgement so.

He closed the distance between us, scooped up my cold rigid fingers, and kissed them. I snatched them back but refrained from wiping them on my skirts. Openly insulting him would probably be a bad idea.

"Welcome, Allaigna." He took me by both shoulders, held me at arm's length, and turned me back and forth. "You make a pretty boy, but an even prettier girl."

I snorted, as indelicately as possible. I would not give in to his pretence of courtesy. "What is it you wished to discuss? I haven't had time to do more translation since this afternoon."

He smiled, undeterred, and pulled out a chair. "Sit. Please share the board with me."

I did sit, arms crossed, legs akimbo, still as ungirlish as possible.

It seemed to amuse him, for he chuckled while he brought over the flagon of wine, the platter of quail, and a loaf of bread.

I accepted the glass of wine but barely let it wet my lips. I could tell from the touch on my tongue it was an excellent vintage, velvety and rich, tasting of honey and oak. It would have come from the warm south of Brandishear, not our cool and rocky vineyards here in Aerach. I wasn't at all hungry, but I took some bread and one of the bony little birds. I might be glad of a full belly later.

Later. How much later? I had hoped to be gone by now, before having to dress in this unwieldy costume and dance this dangerous galliard. Had I been wrong to put my trust in Rhoan? He had convinced me to wait till night to leave the castle, but every nerve in my body wanted out of here now.

Doniver was saying something, and I'd missed most of it. I pretended to be focussed on extricating slivers of meat from the twiggy bones of the quail. It seemed it was just more pleasantries, at least until his hand reached across the round table and grasped my wrist, not hard, but not gently either.

He was leaning forward, eyes sharp and menacing. "I asked, do you know how much you cost me?"

I blinked, unsure how to answer

"You haven't been listening, have you?"

There wasn't much I could say to that without proving it true. "You mean the pigs?"

Apparently, yes, that was it. He leaned closer. He must have been drinking before my arrival. His breath was rank with it, and his pupils were dilated.

"If you weren't such a useful little catch, I would send you back and collect the reward."

I leaned away, narrowing my nostrils against the boozy, animal smell of him. "I thought my information was barely helpful to you."

He laughed, dropping my wrist. "Yes, you're rather useless as a spy. But your worth as a wife will seal the fortunes of this house. How old are you?"

"Fourteen."

"Old enough to be married by the old laws."

I set my jaw and pulled a drumstick off of the quail, perhaps more violently than necessary. "Sixteen is the legal age of marriage in Aerach."

"Common law allows for marriage younger than that, if the parties are in agreement."

Agreement he would never get from me.

"A messenger arrived from your father today."

I froze, the quail drumstick partway to my lips.

"It seems after only two weeks, they've given up on you. They returned the bride price and annulled the betrothal."

My heart soared, then crashed, fluttering to the ground as he continued. "No one is looking for you anymore, Allaigna. You could rot in my dungeons and no one would be the wiser."

His hand was on my wrist once more. He plucked the half-eaten bird leg from my fingers and dropped it on the plate.

"Such a tiny hand," he said. "Worth so much, and so little. It seems to me, Allaigna, you could stay as a guest in my prison, or marry me now."

I pulled back, but he held my wrist firm. "I'll never agree," I hissed, standing.

He followed me, brushing half the food from the table with a clatter.

"Sorry, but you owe me too much to deny me now." As I

retreated, he followed, till my back was to the sideboard. "The old laws will also allow for marriage if you're with child."

Terror stopped my ears, filled my head with rushing blood. His voice was an odd tonal buzzing, too close yet high above me, a distant droning of wasps. The hand that grasped my jaw, forcing my face up, was sweaty, hot, and implacable. I could feel his meaningless words vibrate through his bones and into mine.

I caught the buzz in my throat and enlarged it, letting it swell, tuning the distant drone into a note so large it filled my head and ricocheted off the bones of my jaw, my nose, my brow, propagating subharmonics and overtones as it grew.

His other hand still held my wrist, but now it was wrapped around my back, crushing me against him so he had to bend me backward to bring his face near mine.

As his mouth, still moving in meaningless pantomime, met my lips, I released the sound. It wasn't a song or charm I'd practised or planned: just a raw explosion of panicked energy that ripped from my throat.

He hurtled backward as if hit by a cannonball. His hand nearly snapped my jaw as it went, and the other one, still holding my wrist, dragged me with him.

I landed on top, staring down into unblinking eyes. I struggled to my feet warily, ready to dash for the door if he rose. As I stood, his head rolled to the side, and from a hole no bigger than an arrow shaft in the back of his head, a small puddle of blood began to grow.

§

Allaigna will return in Pulp Literature *Issue 19, Summer 2018.*

Allaigna's Song
Overture

JM Landels

THE ARTISTS

AKEM
Cover artist, Windseeker

Akem forgot she was an illustrator and writer for a few years and is making up for lost time. Her first picture book, a myth about before we were born, is in progress. Her painting *Seabus* was the cover for *Pulp Literature* Issue 16, Autumn 2017. You can find more of her fantasy illustrations at akemiart.ca.

BEN BALDWIN
Illustrators, 'Bone Dry'

Ben Baldwin is a self-taught freelance artist from the UK who works with a combination of traditional media, photography, and digital art programs. He has been shortlisted for the British Fantasy Award for Best Artist for the last seven years and has also been shortlisted for the British Science Fiction Association Award for Best Artist. In 2013, he won Best Artist of the Year in the annual This Is Horror Awards. Look for his painting Jinn later this year on the cover of *Pulp Literature* Issue 20. In the meantime, you can find out more about Ben and his work at benbaldwin.co.uk and facebook.com/pages/Ben-Baldwin/343132594365.

PULP *Literature*

Mel Anastasiou

In-house illustrator

Mel Anastasiou loves drawing for *Pulp Literature* because she loves the stories she illustrates. She draws in black and white, working from imagination and inspired by details from Renaissance compositions. You can find more illustrations, as well as writing tips and news about her books and novellas at melanastasiou.wordpress.com.

JM Landels

Illustrator, Allaigna's Song: Aria

JM Landels studied at the Cartoon Centre in London, UK, under David Lloyd (*V for Vendetta*) and Dougie Braithwaite (*Punisher*). Although she is a perennial doodler, she put down her pencils and brushes after giving birth to three children, but rapidly dusted them off when she realized *Pulp Literature* was going to be an illustrated magazine. She blogs sporadically at jmlandels.stiffbunnies.com.

HALL OF FAME

These are the heroes — the Patrons and Pulp Literati whose monthly support helped bring you this issue. Please lift your glasses and give them a rousing cheer!

The Landlords
Adam Fout

The Innkeepers
Ada Maria Soto
Dana Tye Rally
Ev Bishop
Roger & Anne Anastasiou
Loucas Raptis
A Bursewicz
Kevin Harris

The Cicerones
Sandra Vander Schaaf

The Bartenders
Keith Rydstrom
Alana Krider
David Salcido
Richard Gropp
Angela Dorsey
Margot Landels

Ron Graves
Susan Lefeaux
Cathryn Udesen Parker
Kristen Mah
Corey Reid
Michelle Balfour
Robert Bose
Sharon McAuley
Victoria McAuley
Brighde Moffat
Dave Wayne
Scott F Gray
Abigail Bruce

The Regulars
CC Humphreys
Marta Salek
Rina Piccolo
Leigh Matthews
Kim Harbridge
KT Wagner
Harmony Neal

Jenny Blackford
Jain Cairns
Catherine McArdle
Adelene Ellenberg
Lisa Gordon
Clarisa Rivera Starr
Michael Barrie
Exprmntle
Tom Jolly
Dave Charpentier
Leo X Robertson
Kristene Perron
Akemi Art
Kerry

The Clientele
Kathy Denton
Farideh Shabanfar
Ray Hsu
Melissa Hudson
Andrea Smith
Flo Golod

If you would like to join the ranks of these worthies you can become a patron on Patreon at patreon.com/pulplit, or join the Pulp Literati through our website at pulpliterature.com/join-pulp-literati/.

MARKETPLACE

Books

Allaigna's Song: Overture *by JM Landels.* Music, magic, and the shaping of a hero. pulpliterature.com/allaignas-song-overture

Paperboy: A Dysfunctional Novel *by Bob Thurber.* Photography by Vincent Louis Carrella. shantiarts.co/uploads/files/thurber_paperboy.html

Stella Ryman and the Fairmount Manor Mysteries *by Mel Anastasiou.* Trapped in a down-at-the-heels care home. You'd be cranky too. pulpliterature.com/stella-ryman-and-the-fairmount-manor-mysteries

Trolls *by Kris Sayer.* A comic guidebook narrated by a giant-spoon-wielding troll hunter. tatterhood.bigcartel.com

The Writer's Boon Companion *by Mel Anastasiou.* Thirty Days Towards an Extraordinary Volume. pulpliterature.com/subscribe/the-bookstore

CORPSE DOOR

tatterhood.bigcartel.com

Bookstores

Book Warehouse 632 Broadway W, Vancouver, BC V5Z IGI (604) 872-5711 bookwarehouse.ca

The Comicshop 3518 W 4th Ave, Vancouver, BC V6R IN8 (604) 738-8122 thecomicshop.ca

Myth Hawker Travelling Bookstore Canadian authors•Canadian content•small and independent press mythhawker.ca

Phoenix On Bowen 992 Dorman Rd, Bowen Island, BC V0N IG0 (604) 947-2793

People's Co-op Bookstore 1391 Commercial Dr, Vancouver, BC V5L 3X5 (604) 253-6442 coopbks@telus.net

Dear Geist...

I have been writing and rewriting a creative non-fiction story for about a year. How do I know when the story is ready to send out?

—*Teetering, Gimli MB*

Which is correct, 4:00, four o'clock or 1600 h?
—Floria, Windsor ON

Dear Geist,
In my fiction writing workshop, one person said I should write a lot more about the dad character. Another person said that the dad character is superfluous and I should delete him. Both of these writers are very astute. Help!

—Dave, Red Deer AB

Advice for the Lit-Lorn

Are you a writer?
Do you have a writing question, conundrum, dispute, dilemma, quandary or pickle?

Geist offers free professional advice to writers of fiction, non-fiction and everything in between, straight from Mary Schendlinger (Senior Editor of *Geist* for 25 years) and *Geist* editorial staff.

Send your question to advice@geist.com.

We will reply to all answerable questions, whether or not we post them.

geist.com/lit-lorn

GEIST
FACT · FICTION · NORTH of AMERICA

Regent Bookstore 5800 University Blvd, Vancouver, BC V6T 2E4 (604) 228-1820 regentbookstore.com

Village Books & Coffeeshop 130-12031 First Ave, Richmond, BC V7E 3M1 (604) 272-6601 villagebooks@shaw.ca

White Dwarf/Dead Write Books 3715 West 10th Ave, Vancouver, BC V6R 2G5 (604) 228-8223 whitedwarf@deadwrite.com

"Myth Hawker has a crush on the underdog: the small press, the overlooked author, the independent bookstore, and the vast, undiscovered treasures of small-scale publishing."

Myth Hawker travels the length & breadth of Canada, popping up at conventions & festivals in every province, showcasing the work of small press & independent Canadian authors. Follow them online to see where they're popping up next!

www.mythhawker.com   **@Mythhawker**

Conferences and Events

SiWC at Sea Caribbean Writing Cruise 7-15 April 2018 siwc.ca

Creative Ink Festival for writers, artists & readers 18-20 May 2018·Burnaby, BC Creativeinkfestival.com

MAGAZINES

Geist Ideas + Culture·Made in Canada
geist.com

Mystery Weekly Magazine
The cutting edge of short mystery fiction
www.mysteryweekly.com

Neo-opsis Canadian magazine of science
fiction, based in Victoria, BC neo-opsis.ca

OnSpec The Canadian magazine of the
fantastic onspecmag.wordpress.com

Polar Borealis Paying market for new Canadian SF&F writers & artists polarborealis.ca

Room Magazine Literature, Art, and
Feminism since 1975 roommagazine.com

PRINTING & PUBLISHING

First Choice Books/Victoria Bindery
Book printing & binding·graphic design·
eBooks·marketing materials 1-800-957-
0561·firstchoicebooks.ca

Wesbrook Bay Publishing Beverley Boissery
author and publisher wesbrookbay.com

CONTESTS

Pulp Literature runs four annual contests for poetry, flash fiction, and short stories. For contest guidelines, prizes and entry fees, see our website, pulpliterature.com/contests.

The Magpie Award for Poetry
Contest opens: 1 March 2018
Deadline: 15 April 2018
Winner notified: 15 May 2018
Winner published in: Issue 20, Autumn 2018
Prize: $500

The Hummingbird Flash Fiction Prize
Contest opens: 1 May 2018
Deadline: 15 June 2018
Winner notified: 15 July 2018
Winner published in: Issue 21, Winter 2019
Prize: $300

The Raven Short Story Contest
Contest opens: 1 September 2018
Deadline: 15 October 2018
Winner notified: 15 November 2018
Winner published in: Issue 22, Spring 2019
Prize: $300

THE BUMBLEBEE FLASH FICTION CONTEST
Contest opens: 1 January 2019
Deadline: 15 February 2019
Winner notified: 15 March 2019
Winner published in: Issue 23, Summer 2019
Prize: $300

ℬECOME A PATRON OF PULP LITERATURE!

By supporting *Pulp Literature* on Patreon with $2 or more per month, you will be laying the foundation for a secure future for the magazine, as well as ensuring you will never miss an issue! Your subscription includes four big issues of short stories, novellas, poetry, comics and novel excerpts delivered to your door or electronic mailbox each year.

Find us at patreon.com/pulplit
If you prefer to subscribe through our website go to pulpliterature. com/subscribe.

Or you can send a cheque with the form below to:
Subscriptions
Pulp Literature Press
8540 Elsmore Road, Richmond, BC V7C 2AI, Canada

....

Don't miss an issue!

❏ **Send me 2 years (8 issues) at the special rate of $90** (save $30)*
❏ **Send me 1 year (4 issues) for $50** (save $10)*
❏ **Send me 2 years of digital issues for $30** (save $9.92)
❏ **Send me 1 year of digital issues for $17.50** (save $2.47)

Name: _____
Address: _____
City: _____ Prov. / State: _____
Postal code: _____ Country:_____
Email: _____

❏ Payment enclosed
❏ Bill me
❏ New
❏ Renewal

Make cheques payable in Canadian funds to S. Pieters. Include email address for digital editions and Paypal billing, or subscribe at www.pulpliterature.com.

*for postage outside Canada add $16 per year in North America or $32 per year overseas.